DRAGONS –
AND DECISIONS

To Matthew

Jenny Sullivan

love

Jenny Sullivan

x

PONT

To my husband
Rob
with all my love.

First Impression—2003

ISBN 1 84323 208 1

Printed in Wales at
Gomer Press, Llandysul, Ceredigion

LIST OF CHARACTERS

Tanith Williams	Aged seventeen
Gwydion	Formerly a white cat – but also a Shapeshifter. Now Dragonking of Ynys Haf
Teleri Angharad Probert	Tanith's best friend – known as T.A.
Mam	Tanith's mother
The Ant	Chief Daughter of the Moon – Tanith's Aunt Antonia (and five other Aunts, who, together with Tanith, form the Circle of Seven)
Mr Howard	Once Tanith's School Music Teacher, who is also Taliesin, Bard and Friend to Great Merlin – but only in Ynys Haf
Heledd	Tanith's older sister
Cariad	Heledd's daughter (who bears watching in future…)
Aunty Fliss	Tanith's Aunt Felicity, now living in Ynys Haf to escape the effects of Alzheimer's Disease, a terrible illness which only affects her in the Real Time world
Iestyn	Aunty Fliss's husband and leader of the Ynys Haf community
Nest	Gwydion's Half-Tylwyth Teg Aunt who lives in Ynys Haf
O'Liam of the Green Boots	A Leprechaun
Gwyddno Garanhir	Lord of the Sixteen Doomed Cities of Cantre'r Gwaelod
Elffin	His son (for whom T.A. has rather a soft spot)

Merch Corryn Du Spiderwitch – the Wickedest Witch of all, and Astarte Perkins's (see *The Magic Apostrophe* and other earlier books in the series) Great-Great-Ever-so-many-Greats Grandmother.

Conor   The sinister Leprechaun King, Lord of of the Land Beneath

Maebh   A beautiful but rather dim Irish Princess, great-great-great-grand-daughter of the Spiderwitch.

Master Henbane Maebh's 'minder' – who is using her to gain control of Ynys Haf

Now, I should really, really like to give you a brief run-down of the story so far – but I'm afraid, after eight books, the whole thing has got rather above itself. If you've missed any, here they are:

1

What on earth were we going to do? I mean, when I even thought about it, it made me go cold all over.

For a start, we'd conned Conor of the Land Beneath out of his prey, because we had the real, live Maebh and he had a fake-Maebh. We had O'Liam of the Green Boots and his bride-to-be, Siobhan Flowerface free and clear – but O'Liam had promised to go back once a year for a month and a day to find iron for the leprechaun king, and Conor still had O'Liam's ancient Mammy as hostage. Unfortunately, Conor isn't the sort of person who'd worry about someone being ancient if he wanted revenge!

Oh, we thought we'd been so smart, me and Gwydion – but now we'd been neatly check-mated, because that pea-brain of a best friend of mine, T.A., had talked Gwyddno Garanhir's son-and-heir into jaunting across the Middlesome Sea. They'd gone to find us, we'd missed them entirely, and now Conor had them in his evil clutches.

To make matters even worse, we still had to sort out Ynys Haf, which was being savaged by a terrible drought, and we couldn't discover what – or who – was causing it. I didn't think it was Conor, he'd denied all knowledge, but then, it would be crazy to trust the Leprechaun King and his clever promises.

I didn't know where to start. It was like needing a piece of string long enough to wrap a good-sized parcel, and only having a tangled ball of it with loads of loose ends sticking out, and not knowing which one to pull to unravel it. If we pulled the wrong one, we might be in an even worse mess than ever.

Except a worse mess was hard to imagine.

Gwyddno Garanhir, considering his blue-eyed Elffin had gone missing, was reasonably calm, but Mam Garanhir was anything but. Gwydion was just looking totally hang-dog, Nest was silently chewing the ends of her hair, but I was with Mam Garanhir all the way. When in doubt, panic: that's my motto.

'What are we going to do?' I whinged, jumping out of my chair and pacing up and down Gwyddno's solar where he, Gwydion and I were chewing over the pickle we'd managed to get ourselves into. A whole jarful of pickles, actually. Maebh was being distracted by Lady Garanhir's tiring women, who were helping her try on dresses, while O'Liam was following Siobhan Flowerface around like a moonstruck puppy. Lady Garanhir had been carted off by Elffin's old Nanny, who was patting her hands, giving her sips of something soothing, and calling her 'cariad' and 'ducky' a lot, while Mam Garanhir sniffled and mopped up tears.

Sun poured in through the thick, greenish windows, throwing dappled patterns on the wooden floorboards, but I wasn't into appreciating the décor. My brain was going round like hamster on a wheel, rattling away frantically and not going anywhere at all.

'Panicking isn't going to help,' Gwyddno said reasonably. 'We need to stop and consider our options, and what Conor's reactions are likely to be.'

'What, when he finds out we've foxed him by

giving him a fake Maebh?' I said miserably. 'I don't think he's going to be a happy bunny, somehow.'

'How long is the fake likely to last? When will he find out you tricked him?'

I shrugged. 'Dunno. Could have crumbled to earth and straw five minutes after we left the Land Beneath. It depends on how well the thing was made in the first place. And since it was the first and only time I've ever tried magic that difficult, I doubt that I did much of a job.'

'If we're lucky,' Gwydion said, looking hopeful, 'then maybe we can go back and negotiate with Conor for T.A. and Elffin before the fake-Maebh disintegrates.'

'And if we aren't?' I said, miserably. 'That means Conor has all of us. Then Ynys Haf – and we – are in deep, deep fertiliser.'

Gwyddno Garahnir steepled his fingers and rested his chin on them, gazing unseeingly at me. 'I don't think we have any choice but to go to Erin,' he said after a while. 'We've got to get the youngsters back, and quickly.' He frowned. 'Under normal circumstances, Elffin would be perfectly safe. As my son he has a sort of diplomatic immunity wherever he goes in the Celtic and Gaelic nations, but with what's been going on between you and Conor, and since he was escorting your friend, things are rather different. They might choose to treat him as a spy. I think we'd better get going as soon as we can.'

'Not we,' Gwydion said firmly. 'Tanith and me. Not you, Gwyddno. It's too dangerous to take you. What if Conor captures you, too? That would leave Cantre'r

Gwaelod open to all sorts of problems if neither Elffin or you are here.'

I tugged his sleeve. 'No, it wouldn't, Gwydion.'

'Shut up, Tanz. Who's Dragonking?'

'You are, but if –'

'No, my mind's made up. He stays, we go.'

'Gwydi –'

'I said, leave this to me, Tanz!'

I managed to catch his eye. 'Gwydion, may I have a word in private. Please?' I said pointedly.

'What? Oh, I suppose so. Excuse us a minute, Gwyddno. But you aren't coming, so that's that.'

I tugged Gwydion into the corner of the solar and turned my back on Gwyddno so he couldn't hear what I was saying or read my lips. 'Nothing is going to happen to Gwyddno. Remember the legend? Cantre'r Gwaelod, the sea breaking in, people drowning? I know it''s sad, but it's perfectly safe to take him with us now, because we know he has to be here sometime in the future when that happens, right?'

Gwydion stroked his chin, the bristles rasping under his fingers. 'There's that, I suppose,' he agreed grudgingly. 'But I still don't think we should take him.'

'Elffin's his son, Gwydion, and even though Elffin has blotted his copybook by sticking his nose into Conor's business, Gwyddno is still Lord of Cantre'r Gwaelod and Conor should respect that, right?'

'Who knows what Conor does and doesn't respect?' Gwydion muttered. 'Oh, all right, he can come, I suppose. You can come with us, Gwyddno.'

'I thank you, my lord Dragonking,' Gwyddno said

drily, 'but I was going to anyway, with or without your permission. Elffin is my son.'

'Actually,' I said, my brain finally clicking into gear, 'we have another problem, don't we?'

'We do?' The Dragonking's noble brow furrowed and he started to chew his fingernails.

I slapped his hand down. 'Don't. Bad habit.'

'You do it!'

'Only one fingernail.'

'What problem?'

'Maebh. Remember, she has a vague-ish blood-right to rule Ynys Haf, doesn't she? If you go, and I go, and Gwyddno goes, and anything happens to us, then she can just step in and take over, right? Call herself Queen.'

'Hadn't thought of that,' Gwydion said, sitting down again and resting his elbows on the polished table. 'What do you suggest we do, then?'

I thought about it for a bit. 'Two choices,' I said at last. 'Either take Maebh with us, or leave Gwyddno here as Regent in your place.'

We both turned expectantly to Gwyddno Garanhir, Lord of Cantre'r Gwaelod. He shoved his spectacles up his nose and sighed. 'If you put it like that,' he said, scowling, 'I suppose it's my duty as your liege man to stay and hold the fort, if that's what you want. But my personal opinion is that you should take Maebh with you, and me too. You may have to use her to bargain with. I think you should leave Nest and the Lady's Aunt Flissy as joint Regents in your absence.'

Bargaining with Conor over Maebh? I didn't like the sound of that. We'd promised Maebh we wouldn't hand her over to him. Well, I had, anyway. My sympathy bone had run away with me and so had my big mouth and as usual it had got me into trouble.

'What about O'Liam?' I asked. 'It would be useful to take him: he knows Conor better than anyone, but he's going to be a married leprechaun soon. Will he *want* to come?'

'If I command it,' Gwydion said, pompously, 'he will obey.'

'Oh, get you, Mr Masterful,' I grinned.

He had the grace to blush. 'I wish some people would remember that I deserve *some* respect,' he said plaintively, 'I'm doing my best to rule here.'

I grinned. 'You aren't doing too bad a job, I suppose. In between getting yourself kidnapped and enchanted. But before we all go swanning off to Erin on a rescue mission, there's something else we need to know, desperately.'

'There is?'

'It would be useful if we could find out who, exactly, is behind this curse on Ynys Haf. We know it isn't Master Nasty Henbane, and we know it isn't Conor or Maebh, so, who?'

Gwydion looked at me expectantly. 'Any ideas?'

I subsided. 'Not really. But I think we ought to go back to Castell Du and discuss all this with Flissy and Nest. See if they've got any idea who's causing Ynys Haf all this trouble. Besides, if they're going to rule in your absence, we ought to let them know, right?'

'Right. But all things considered, I think we'll leave Maebh here with Gwyddno for the time being. I don't want her too close to Henbane's dungeon. And

O'Liam is busy making up for lost time courting his Siobhan and I can't bear to tear him away from her. So just us, Tanith, right?'

So, after promising Gwyddno we wouldn't go to Erin without him, Gwydion and I left Cantre'r Gwaelod and took to the skies, heading for Castell Du.

·

2

By the time we got to the *tŷ hir*, it was mid-afternoon, and once we'd eaten and rested, we decided it would be as well to get everyone together who might possibly be able to help us sort out the mess. Since we didn't have ANY ideas at all, whatever anyone could suggest might help!

I suppose the Dragonking and Lady-ish thing to do would have been to send out messengers to command the village head people to come to us. But Gwydion isn't that sort of stuffy person, and neither am I, so Gwydion, Nest, Flissy and I shifted into gulls and went to see them, just as the sun was setting. It was terrible, flying over Ynys Haf these days. There was hardly any green anywhere: crops had withered in the fields, trees were turning brown and leaves were falling, and the sun shone as mercilessly as ever. Even with the sun sinking like a giant red ball over the sea, there was no let up in the unbelievable heat. The rivers had all dried to pathetic trickles, and on the banks lay the skeletons of cows and sheep that had searched in vain for water and fodder. And yet it was barely May, and Ynys Haf should have been just drifting sweetly into summer.

We landed outside the village, and when we had shifted back, Nest suggested that we dress up a bit posh, to make up for the not-summoning bit.

'It's a mistake to be *too* un-royal and approachable, Gwydion,' she said, smoothing down the skirt of her dark green silk dress. 'You are High King after all, and you may need to be a bit fierce some time in the future.'

'All that bossing and bellowing and ordering people about just isn't me, Nest,' Gwydion complained. 'I feel silly throwing my weight about when it isn't necessary.'

'But that's the whole point, Gwydion,' Flissy said. 'If they know you *can* do it, they'll be just that little bit wary of you, and you're less likely to ever to *have* to.'

'It's called psychology, Gwyd,' I said, adjusting the moon-and-stars coronet so that it nestled comfortably on my French-plaited hair. 'You can be as nice as pie, but you need to keep that little bit of distance, a bit of mystery and respect, sort of thing, or when you need to get tough, you won't be able to. They'll just ignore you and do what they want to do.'

'If you say so,' the Dragonking grumbled, straightening the front of his velvet robe. 'But I always feel such a complete prat in this get-up.'

'Nonsense,' Flissy said briskly, reaching up to straighten his collar and pat his cheek, 'you look very nice, dear. You do pay for dressing, as my old Mam used to say.'

'Oh, *very* respectful,' I sniggered, and was rewarded with a look from Gwydion that would have given an Eskimo chilblains.

When we were ready, we swept majestically into the village. A small boy saw us coming and ran around shrieking at the top of his voice that the Dragonking had arrived. Iestyn, Flissy's husband and head-man in the village and Eifion Gwyn, his deputy, bustled out to meet us. By the time they'd escorted us to the longhouse that served as the community's meeting-place, the villagers were assembling.

Assorted children lurked at the back of the long, smoky hall, and I was glad to see Branwen among them, her coppery hair glowing in the evening light through the windows. A woman brought us earthenware goblets of mead, and the villagers stopped fidgeting and stared at us expectantly.

Gwydion took a sip and set down his goblet. 'Thank you for your welcome,' he said, humbly. 'I know I haven't been much –'

The idiot's going to apologise, I thought, suddenly. *For being a lousy Dragonking or something, when he isn't, not at all.* I jumped straight in, not thinking twice. And yes, I know that's got me into trouble before, but this was instinct, all right?

'He's trying to say,' I interrupted smoothly, 'that he's sorry that the business of being Dragonking has taken him away from Ynys Haf just when our country is suffering from this terrible drought. But now he's here to ask for your help.'

Gwydion frowned and opened his mouth, and on his left I saw Nest's arm move to dig him firmly in the ribs to shut him up. He closed it again.

'Even I, Tan'ith, your Lady, and the Moonwitch Rhiannon' (which is Flissy's Circle of Seven name, of course), 'are helpless to lift the spell.'

'Thought you wuz the most powerful witch of all,' Sion ap Sion muttered, just loud enough for me to hear him. 'Little fussy spotty dapple thing, not as clever as you thought you was. Always knew it, I did!'

16

Flissy heard him too, which was just as well, because she jumped in just in time to prevent me from marmalising the little creep.

'Even the most powerful witch cannot remove a spell, Sion ap Sion,' she thundered, 'until she knows how it was cast.'

'We thought at first it was Conor of the Land Beneath,' Gwydion put in, having recovered his voice, 'but it wasn't.'

'And you believed a leppercorn? Can't trust no sneaky leppercorns,' Sion ap Sion muttered mutinously. 'Prob'ly 'im all along, no matter what he do say.'

'Usually I would agree,' I said icily, giving him my best Hard Stare, 'but on this occasion I believe him. He had no reason to lie.'

'Leppercorns don't need no reason to lie, they don't. They just goes and does it for the fun of it. Nasty, sneaky –'

'Be quiet, Sion ap Sion.' Iestyn's exasperated voice silenced the plump little man. 'If our Dragonking and the Lady both think it wasn't Conor, then it wasn't, all right? So just shut up and let them speak.'

Flissy nodded her approval of her husband's intervention. 'Thank you, Iestyn. Shall we all listen to the Dragonking and the Lady now?'

All eyes turned to Gwydion and me, sitting side by side on our wooden bench – the only one in the room with a back to it.

'I know it's going back a fair while,' Gwydion began, 'but did anyone notice anything out of the ordinary around the time the drought started?'

'Apart from the torrential rain and gales, Castell Du and Castell y Ddraig gettin' captured, great monstrous ravening beasts with fangs and claws and stuff roamin' all over the place, that woman Maebh, that slimy Master Henbane, Rhiryd ap Rhiryd Goch and them rotten twins pitchin' up, you mean?' Sion ap Sion said sarcastically.

I sighed. As usual, the little man with the handlebar moustache was beginning to annoy me. He had a real talent for it. 'Exactly,' I said smoothly, favouring him with my killer glare. 'Apart from *that*, which *everybody* knows all about. So, did anyone notice anything? Anything at all that might help save Ynys Haf?'

The villagers looked at each other, frowning and whispering, and there was a lot of head-shaking and pursed lips and sucking of hollow teeth. Looked as if we were going to draw a blank. Then, out of the corner of my eye, I caught sight of a sudden movement at the back of the room, where a cluster of excited children stood. I glanced across and met Branwen's eyes. The little red-haired girl was hopping from foot to foot, biting her lip, but it wasn't because she wanted to go to the loo. I could tell from the expression on her face that she had something to say.

I concentrated very hard, letting my magic flow towards her, wrapped it around her middle, very gently lifted her up into the air and over the heads of the assembled villagers, and set her down beside me. I patted the bench, and Gwydion scooted over to make room for her between us.

Her eyes shone like Christmas morning. 'Ooh,

Lady,' she breathed, 'oooh, Lady, you flew me, you flew me!'

Eifion Gwyn, her father, sitting in the front row, groaned. 'You'm spoiling my girl, Lady,' he complained. 'She'm getting impossible, what with you making so much of her, she is! Needs a good hiding, that's what!'

'I'm not spoiling her at all,' I retorted. 'She's a very brave little girl. If it hadn't been for Branwen raising the alarm when Rhiryd ap Rhiryd invaded the castle, then goodness knows what might have happened. The Dragonking might be dead. And so might you!'

Branwen glanced nervously at her furious father. 'I'm not brave, Lady,' she whispered, the freckled little face worried, 'I'm a terrible girl, my Dada says.'

I bent down and whispered in her ear. 'Me, too, Branwen,' I said, winking at her, 'my Dada says the same about me – and he's probably right. Nothing wrong with being a terrible girl if it gets the job done.'

She blushed with pleasure, and snuggled a little closer, careful not to look at her father.

I turned back to the villagers. 'Dragonson asked you all a question a while ago,' I said. 'And I think Branwen has something to say. Have you, Branwen? Don't be shy.'

She nodded, and glanced under her lashes at Gwydion. 'As long as Gwydion Dragonking won't be cross with me,' she said timidly.

'He won't,' I assured her. 'He'll be too busy being grateful, trust me. Go on, tell us.'

'The dragon,' Branwen said shyly. 'The one the Dragonking calls Bugsy. I made friends with him.'

Eifion Gwyn leapt to his feet, his white eyebrows drawn together. 'I thought I told you to stay away from that nasty, scaly creature!' he bellowed. 'Just you wait until I get you home, my girl!'

Branwen burst into tears. 'He's not a nasty creature! He's lonely, and he's been trying to tell Gwydion something for ages, but first Gwydion was wounded, and then he was off to the Land across the Middlesome Sea, so he hasn't been listening,' she sobbed.

I patted her back and gave her my hanky – she was about to wipe her nose on her sleeve. 'Come on, Branwen. Just tell us, all right?'

She nodded, avoiding her father's furious face. 'All right, Lady. See, I can talk to him.'

Gwydion's mouth dropped open. 'You can *what?*'

'I can talk to him. Not with my voice, but sort of with my mind,' the child went on shyly. 'I can hear what he's thinking, and he can hear what I'm thinking.'

'Rubbish!' Eifion Gwyn snapped. 'Girls don't think at all, they don't, so how could anybody hear them? Bad enough when they do talk, let alone makin' out they do think!'

'I do think!' Branwen burst out. 'I think a lot. I'm not stupid, Dada!'

'Indeed you aren't,' Flissy soothed. 'What did Bugsy have to say?'

'He's very sad. He says he's let Gwydion Dragonking down. Dragonking gave him a job to do, and he disobeyed him.'

Gwydion looked puzzled. 'Job?' he murmured.

'What job?' Then he remembered. 'I told him to get rid of Spiderwitch,' he groaned. 'You mean he didn't?'

Branwen shook her head. 'He kept her. He thought she'd make a nice pet.'

I stared at Gwydion. 'Spiderwitch? *A nice pet?*'

'Just accept that you don't know how dragons' minds work, Tanz,' Gwydion said weakly. 'If he wasn't a thousand times my size, I'd smack his tail for him.'

'That's why he's been flying over the castle and stuff all the time,' Branwen explained. 'He was trying to get you to notice him and follow him. But you didn't. He said you aren't any more –' she stopped suddenly and went bright red.

'Any more what?' Gwydion asked, scowling.

Branwen shook her head, refusing to speak.

I put my head down to her level. 'Go on, whisper.'

A tiny, embarrassed voice muttered hotly in my ear. 'Bugsy says Dragonking isn't any more intelligent now than when he was a boy and Bugsy was trying to train him.'

When I stopped giggling and saw Gwydion's indignant face, I decided it was time to get back into Lady mode again.

'What Branwen has told us,' I said, 'will help us find Merch Corryn Du, the Spiderwitch, and get rid of her once and for all. We won't let her escape this time. Perhaps now we can begin to break the spell on Ynys Haf.'

We thanked Iestyn Mawr and the villagers, and got ready to leave. But I saw the expression on Eifion Gwyn's face, and knew that Branwen would be for it as soon as we left. Flissy had already told me that Eifion's wife had died, so Branwen had no Mam to protect her. No doubt about it, she was in for a walloping. So I made an Executive Decision (I can do those, now I'm the Lady)!

'Branwen shall come with us,' I said imperiously, waving my hand. 'I have decided she shall be my – um – secretary.'

'Seckertry?' Eifion Gwyn bellowed. 'What's a seckertry when it's at home?'

'Someone who looks after my correspondence and is generally helpful,' I said.

'Her can't read nor write, so fat lot of good she's goin' to be as a whatchamacallit? A *seckertry!*' Eifion Gwyn sneered. 'Ha!'

'I shall teach her all she needs to know,' I said smugly. I thought, *So there, smarty-pants*, but I had more sense than to say it. And we left, taking Branwen with us.

3

When I shape-shifted Branwen back at the *tŷ hir*, however, I saw that her face was pink beneath the freckles, and her lower lip looked a bit wobbly. I bent my knees so that my face was on a level with hers. 'What's up, sunshine?' I asked.

'Ooh, Lady,' she squeaked, dizzy after being moused and carried from the village, 'I think our Dada's going to be furious when I'm not there to make his supper!'

'Your Dada's going to have to put up with it, Branwen,' I said, 'learn to make his own cheese-on-toast!' Then Flissy poked me in the back. Was I missing something here? I tried to remember being eight years old, and the something clicked. 'But you can always go back, whenever you want,' I assured her. 'Just because I'd like you to help me doesn't mean you can't ever go back to see him. I'm not kidnapping you, you know!' I was rewarded with a huge beam of relief. 'Any time you want,' I repeated. 'Just say the word, all right? I'll have you there before you can say collywobbles.'

She nodded vigorously, her amber plaits bobbing, and then Flissy went into surrogate Mam mode, and bustled her away.

Next day, Gwydion, Nest and I sat around the wooden table.

'A pet Spiderwitch, eh,' Gwydion said. 'Who'd have thought Bugsy would do anything so stupid?'

'Not knowing too much about dragons,' I said

mildly, 'I couldn't possibly comment. Aren't dragons supposed to be fierce, and rather fond of barbecuing people?'

'Bugsy's different,' Gwydion fiddled with the little earthenware pot of salt on the table. 'I had him when he was just out of the egg, and he sort of thinks he's human. He and Fang –'

'Fang?' I put in. 'Who's Fang?'

'Fang was my dog. I rescued him from your Time, and brought him back. He and Bugsy were great friends, but dogs don't live as long as dragons, even in Ynys Haf. He was about 200 when he died, and that's our years, not dog ones, but – well, I think Bugsy misses him. Probably misses me, too, since I became Dragonking. I've been a bit preoccupied, what with one thing and another. Maybe that's why he decided to keep Merch Corryn Du. He was lonely.'

'So, what do we do?' Nest asked.

Gwydion sighed. 'Go up the mountain and find Bugsy, I suppose,' he suggested. 'And take his pet away. I don't think he's going to be too happy with us, mind.'

I don't think he'd thought things through properly. 'If she's still up there with Bugsy – which is a really stupid name for a dragon, if you want my opinion – then how come she's managed to work enough magic to harm Ynys Haf so badly?' I asked.

'I was wondering that, too,' Nest agreed. 'But there's only one way to find out. Go and talk to Bugsy.'

'There's a bit of a problem with that,' Gwydion said, frowning, 'I can't talk Dragon. I tried to learn, but I couldn't get the hang of it at all. Can't speak it, can't understand it. Altogether too many consonants, especially X's and Z's, and the fiery burps don't help. Merlin says he understands it, but I'm not sure I actually believe him. So what do we do now?'

I grinned. Then, 'Branwen,' I called. The little girl came at a run.

'Yes, Lady?' she asked, hopping from foot to foot excitedly.

'When you want to talk to Bugsy,' I asked, 'how do you get hold of him? Do you go looking?'

'Yes Lady,' she said. 'If my Dada don't want me home, doing stuff, I climb the mountain and see if I can find him. Sometimes, mind, he flies over and sees me, and then we stop and have a bit of a chat. Well, not exactly a chat, Lady, more a bit of a *think* together.'

'Do you think he'd talk to us if you came with us?'

She nodded, her eyes wide and blue as sunny puddles. 'It's a long climb, Lady, but I'm sure he'd talk to you. He's been trying to talk to Gwydion Dragonking for ages, but he wouldn't pay any attention, so he's a bit cross with him. But I expect he'll talk to *you*.'

'Won't be a long climb, Branwen,' I assured her. 'How would you like to learn to fly?'

She was a good pupil: within minutes of being airborne, Branwen-the-red-kite was perfectly in control of her wings, soaring and squeaking with excitement. She just missed flying into a tree, then settled down sensibly, her eyes shining with joy.

Gwydion, Nest and I flew with her in formation,

soaring across country and up into the wild peaks of Snowdonia. The air was cooler over the mountains, but the drought was gradually creeping up the slopes, and because there had been no rain, the secret lakes were slowly evaporating, shrinking, and the sky they reflected was a harsh, unhealthy yellow.

A dragon Bugsy's size doesn't take much finding, even in Eryri: we spotted him a fair distance off, perched on a crag, glooming down the valley, his long, scaly neck curved.

He was much bigger than the last time I'd seen him. Then, he had flapped in, picked up Spiderwitch in one terrible talon, and carried her off. His wingspan now must have been about the size of a jumbo jet, and the muscular haunches were approximately the size of a double-decker bus – each! The fierce points along his back bristled, and his talons – well, you probably don't want to know. They'd probably give you nightmares.

He was huge, and so still that I thought he was sleeping, but then I saw a slitted golden eye gleam behind the half-closed lid, and knew he was as aware of us as we were of him. We flew in to land in front of him, and I really, really hoped he was in a good mood. He could frizzle us before we had a chance to shape-shift, if he felt like it. I shifted Branwen first. Seemed like a good idea, since they were buddies, right? As the child shimmered into her own shape, Bugsy's eyes opened, the great head lifted, and he curved his huge neck until his head was on a level with her. I'd swear he was smiling . . .

Branwen drew back her fist and punched him with all her might between the eyes. I winced, expecting

26

her to be vaporised at any second, but the dragon nudged her gently, making her stagger back, and she did it again. Then she wrapped both arms around his head and hugged him. I suppose a thump like that is a love-pat to a dragon!

By this time the rest of us had shifted. Gwydion waited patiently until the beast had finished his little love-in with Branwen.

The child let go of the dragon and rested her forehead against his, affectionately. Then she giggled, covering her mouth with her hand, and flashed a quick look at Gwydion.

'What?' I asked, but she shook her head, giggling harder.

'Ooh, I daren't say, Lady!' she said, her grin stretching from ear to ear.

'You're the only one who can talk to him, Branwen,' I said sternly, 'it's your solemn duty to tell us exactly what he says!'

She spluttered, and looked at Gwydion under her eyelashes, grabbed hold of the end of her plait and chewed it.

'Come on, Branwen,' I ordered. 'Tell us!' I had a feeling this was going to be good.

'Bugsy says,' she said, going pink, 'that it's about time Gwydion Dragonking paid attention to what was going on around him. He said –' she stopped. 'Ooh, I can't, Lady!'

'Yes, you can!'

'Bugsy says that if the Dragonking had visited him occasionally instead of gadding about after the Irish female person, Ynys Haf wouldn't be in this state.'

Gwydion bristled. 'And neither would it be if Bugsy the Dragon had done as he was told and got rid of Spiderwitch, either.'

'O.K., O.K.,' I butted in, hastily, before this turned into a slanging match – or worse. 'Both of you are at fault. Now apologise nicely, Gwydion, and let's see what we can find out.'

'*Me,* apologise?' Gwydion muttered. 'Wasn't me who decided to keep some evil old witch for a *pet*, was it?'

Bugsy gently nudged Branwen aside, and let out a tiny lick of flame that (rather pointedly, I thought), singed the toe of Gwydion's left boot.

'All right, all right, I'm sorry!' he yelped, dancing back hastily. 'All my fault. Should have been specific, right?'

The dragon nodded, ponderously.

Branwen put out her hand and patted the great face. 'He says he's sorry, too. He didn't think the Spiderwitch would get away from where he left her, but she did.'

'What?' Nest groaned, 'I was afraid of that. So she's escaped?'

Bugsy nodded again.

'She waited until he was –' Branwen blushed again, and darted a glance at me. 'Bugsy was courting, Lady. There's a lady dragon in the next valley, and he was a bit occupied one night, and the Spiderwitch disappeared. He looked and looked for her, but then the terrible storms began. He wasn't sure at first if they were her fault, but then, when Ynys Haf began to dry up, he knew it was Spiderwitch who was doing it. He says he's been flying over your camp in the mountains night after night, trying to tell you, but you ignored him.'

'I didn't ignore him!' Gwydion protested. 'I saw him, but how did I know he wanted to talk to me?'

The dragon and Branwen touched foreheads again. Branwen giggled nervously. 'Bugsy says you never were terribly bright.'

Gwydion scowled. 'Now look here, Bugsy, just because I don't speak Dragon very well – oh, all right, not at all – it doesn't mean I'm stupid!'

Bugsy the dragon raised one huge, terribly expressive eyebrow.

'Now look, you two,' I said hastily, 'shouldn't we be trying to sort out what we're going to do about Spiderwitch? She's more important than a silly argument. So stop bickering.'

Bugsy gave me what seemed to be an approving look, and lowered the eyebrow. He bent his head to Branwen again.

'Bugsy says he thinks he might know where she is. Or at least, he says he thinks he knows where she's been.'

'Will you take us there,' Gwydion asked, fairly humbly for him, 'please, Bugsy?'

I'll swear that dragon grinned. He gathered his haunches together beneath the vast body, spread his wings with a leathery, creaky noise, and shoved off the mountain top, circling impatiently while we shifted ourselves and Branwen. Then he swooped down on currents of hot air, gliding parallel with the side of the crag, with us hurtling after him, buffeted by his slipstream.

He flew for a while, and then landed on the side of a mountain on a flat piece of land. A wizened tree grew sideways out of the rock, and beside the gnarled roots was the black opening of a cave.

We shifted back, shimmering into our human shapes. I noticed that Branwen was getting used to the sudden twiddling of her arms and legs into wings and back: she was getting quite nonchalant about it. That's kids for you, I suppose! She could probably programme a video, too, if they'd been invented!

'In there?' I whispered.

The dragon nodded.

I gulped. It looked dark and rather horrid. I took a deep breath. 'Come on, guys,' I muttered. 'Let's go Spiderwitch-hunting.'

It didn't cheer me at all to see Bugsy reach out a gigantic talon, hook it into Branwen's tunic and pin her gently down so that she couldn't follow us. If the dragon was worried, then . . .

4

Then I probably should be too, right? Right. I mean, I've done a lot of things I didn't particularly want to do while in Lady mode, and this was most definitely another!

To begin with, the cave was dark. Yes, I know that as soon as I got inside I could fix that – I am the Lady, and if I want light, I get light. But I had to get in there, first, and as I said, it was dark with a capital D. I glanced at Gwydion: his face was set in a determined scowl. Oh, great. I knew that look. It was terror.

'Come on,' I said, took a deep breath and got on with it. The reason the cave was so dark was that the entrance was just a half-metre deep: a solid wall of rock was in our way, with just a slim passage leading into the depths of the cavern. Beyond that entrance, only a few steps in, the dark was so dark I couldn't breathe. I screwed my eyes up tight, and concentrated. 'Light,' I said, firmly, and a silvery glow appeared in the air in front of us, a glow that swelled and grew until it was bright as full moonlight – which of course it was. I reached out my hand, and Gwydion took it. Why not? After all, we were both scared. Spiderwitch was Astarte's Great, Great, ever-so-many greats Granny, so she was no sweet little old lady!

There was just room for us to walk side by side, the moonlight bobbing ahead of us, and then I saw that the passageway ahead of us was weirdly misty. At first I couldn't work out what it was, and then I realised that thousands and thousands of spiderwebs spanned the walls and roof . . . Yuk. I may have mentioned before, I don't like spiders. The only good thing about it was that the webs were normal spider size, not Spiderwitch sized. Spiderwitch webs are thick enough to trap a human being – which is what she passes for when she isn't being a spider.

Gwydion swatted down the nearest webs. Spiders of all sizes scuttled for cover, wolf spiders, mesh web spiders, daddy-long-legs, house spiders – huge, huge house spiders, great-grandaddy ones from the look of them; tiny money spiders, garden spiders, everything, in fact, that made a web seemed to have moved into the cavern. I suppose they would: they were her courtiers. She was Queen of Spiders. Now, that was fine by me, but Spiderwitch wanting to be Queen of Ynys Haf? Not on your nelly!

The miniature moon bobbed ahead of us, slipping through the webs as only light can. Ahead, the passageway opened out into a huge cave. Stalagmites and stalactites stretched up and down from floor and ceiling, and from their moist tips a spider web began, stretching across most of the cavernous space. The air was musty, smelling like a mouse-cage that hasn't been cleaned for too long.

O.K., so you aren't afraid of spiders? Well, imagine a spider*web* that is as thick as your wrist, covered in oozy droplets of sticky stuff the size of tennis balls, the web strong enough to hold a full-grown man helpless. Well, that's what was probably ahead of us. Gwydion and I stood silently on the threshold, listening. Silence.

'I don't think she's here,' I whispered. 'I can't hear her.'

I wasn't listening for a voice: I was listening for the hypnotic thrum of long spidery forelegs on that gigantic web. It would have sounded like the low notes of a cello. So she was either keeping very quiet and still, or she wasn't there. I really, really hoped it was the latter. Of course it would have been nice to have met Spiderwitch and zapped her, right at the beginning, so that we could get on with solving our other problems, but if it's all the same to you, I'd rather meet her on our territory, not hers.

'I can't, either,' he whispered back. 'So where is she?'

And then I heard a soft moan, high up above our heads. Gwydion heard it, too, and we stared at each other.

'Do you think that's her?' he whispered.

'I don't know. Doesn't sound like her. Sounds like someone in trouble. Perhaps she's caught someone. Had we better have a look?' Of course, I was hoping he'd say, 'What, us climb up her web? Are you mad?' But he didn't. He nodded, shimmered and shifted into a Gwydion-sized spider. Well, as far as I'm concerned the only thing worse than having spiders all over the place is probably being one: that's a shape-shift too far, so I stayed me. I watched him stretch out his long, creepy front legs and test the web, then begin the long climb up. He disappeared into blackness, and I had to make the choice to keep the light down there with me, or send it after him. Gulp. Oh, go on, then. The moonlight drifted away from me and followed the climbing creature, casting eerie, spidery shadows on the walls. Suddenly the light began to move downward, and Gwydion scuttled after it. I shivered. I was very, very fond of Gwydion – but he was hard to love in this particular shape, and I couldn't wait for him to shift back.

As he stepped off the web, he blurred and the spider disappeared, thank goodness. Then it got worse.

'You're going to have to shift and come with me. I can't manage on my own,' he gabbled.

'What?' I asked, 'what's wrong? Has she caught someone?' I was too late: he'd shifted back. Oh, yuk, yuk, yuk! I had to concentrate really hard to spiderise myself. It was the last pair of legs that did it. And the personality. Spiders don't look like cuddly creatures, and they aren't. It was, next to the mole, quite the savagest mind I'd ever been in. It thought of food, and food, and sinking spidery fangs into more food, and it didn't particularly matter if the food was alive or dead.

I had to concentrate really hard to follow Gwydion up the web. He was halfway up it by the time I'd come to terms with being a spider, so I had to scuttle extra hard to catch up. The moon bobbed with us, and when I saw who was trapped in Spiderwitch's web I could understand why Gwydion was flapping, rather.

Wrapped round with thick ropes of spidersilk, his eyes closed, moaning softly, was Taliesin.

'What's *he* doing here?' I asked, but Gwydion was vainly trying to rip apart the gluey silk ropes to free our friend. I joined in, tried to rip, but the silk was stronger than a ship's hawser. Only one thing for it. Carefully setting my feet (well, one pair of them, the pair that felt like they might be my real ones) between the huge globules of sticky stuff, I shifted again, and

34

magicked myself a pair of twenty-first-century, state of the art bolt-cutters. I know I'm not supposed to magic stuff that isn't already in Ynys Haf, but this was an emergency, and occasionally even the Lady needs to break a rule. I had Taliesin free in a minute or two, and then shifted back. Between us we passed his limp body from strand to strand, careful to avoid the sticky bits, until we were all safely on the ground again. Well, as safe as one can be when the ground in question is in a human-sized, venomous spider's home-sweet-home.

We shifted back and knelt beside Taliesin. I patted his face, and he groaned. His eyes fluttered open and then closed again. 'He's well out of it,' I said. 'We'll have to carry him out.'

Gwydion shifted him to a mouse, which was a bit easier to carry than six feet of unconscious magician. We fairly pelted down the passageway, and ducked round the rock wall into the fresh air, taking huge gulps of it. Even hot and dry as it was, it was much, much better than the stale, musty air inside the cave. Branwen and Bugsy were waiting. The dragon had curled his tail around the little girl and angled one great wing above her, like a bird of prey 'mantling', to shield her from the sun. He lifted his head as we appeared, the elongated black pupils startling in the golden eyes.

'You're back!' Branwen yelled, shoving Bugsy's tail aside and clambering out. 'Did you kill the Spiderwitch?'

I shook my head. 'She wasn't home,' I said, busying myself with the limp little mouse in Gwydion's cupped hands.

Branwen peered at it. 'Oh, poor little thing!' she said sadly, 'is it dead? Did Spiderwitch get it?'

'I hope it isn't,' I said fervently. Branwen squeaked as I shifted the mouse back to Taliesin. He was just as limp as before. 'We need to get him back to the *tŷ hir*, right now, so that Nest and Fliss can have a look at him. I don't know what Spiderwitch has done to him, but he's in a bad way.'

'I don't think it would be a good idea to shift him again so soon,' Gwydion said, worriedly. 'Until we know what's wrong, it's too risky. We got away with it once, but we might scramble his bits and never get them back together again. That's the trouble with magic: when a person has as much of it as Taliesin has, you have to treat it carefully if you're on the outside, if you see what I mean. So how are we going to get him home?'

Branwen went pale. 'Scramble his bits?' she said. Bugsy stretched out his head and nudged her – gently, for a dragon of his size – in the back. When she picked herself up, she turned and put her forehead against the dragon's. A second later, she turned, frowning importantly. 'Bugsy says that if you put the magician on his back, he will carry him for you.'

So we lifted the unconscious figure onto the dragon's broad back – that was difficult enough: Taliesin was limp and heavy – and Gwydion sat astride the scaly creature to hold the magician secure. Then Branwen and I crouched down on the flat space on the mountain while the dragon stretched his wings, flapped once, twice, and was airborne, his huge crimson shape gliding on the thermals rising from the valley. I shifted Branwen and myself back into red kite shape, and we launched ourselves off the rocky plateau and followed Gwydion, Taliesin and Bugsy down into the valley.

We were back at the *tŷ hir* fairly fast, and Bugsy hovered over the trees surrounding the little longhouse. There wasn't enough space for him to land safely, and the trees wouldn't bear his massive weight. Gwydion jumped off, then Bugsy carefully let Taliesin slither off his back, then snagged his belt with a claw as he fell, and lowered him to the ground. Well, nearly. He managed to get to about two metres above ground level, and then dropped him. Gwydion and I broke his fall, but having a large human being fall on you is no joke.

'Oof!' I said, removing his elbow from my solar plexus. Bugsy flapped, rose, and was gone.

Between us we carried Taliesin into the *tŷ hir,* and dumped him on the edge of the wooden platform that held Flissy's wooden chest and cupboard for her herbs and magical stuff. Flissy was outside, pouring washing-up water onto her cabbages – there was too little of the wet stuff around to waste even a drop. She looked hot and tired, and was wiping perspiration off her forehead as she came in through the door.

'Taliesin?' she said, rushing to his side. 'What's he doing here? I thought he was with Merlin, sorting out Guinevere and Arthur in Camelot!'

'So did we,' Gwydion said grimly. 'But we found him stuck in Merch Corryn Du's web, Fliss. I don't know what's wrong with him.'

Fliss put her hand on his forehead, the way Mam-type people do when someone is poorly.

'He's got a bit of a temperature,' she said, frowning. 'He was in the web, you said?'

Gwydion nodded.

'Help me get his shirt off.'

Gwydion lifted up Taliesin's top half while Flissy hauled the baggy white linen shirt over his head. When he was horizontal again, Flissy stared hard at his bare chest.

'No, nothing there. Turn him over, Gwyd.'

Gwydion flipped him over, and Flissy humphed. 'There,' she said, pointing to two large bruises on his left shoulder, a dark red spot in the centre of each. 'Spider venom.'

I felt sick. 'Will he die?'

'If he isn't dead already, then Spiderwitch doesn't want to kill him yet. She was saving him for something. Fresh meat, probably.'

I shuddered. 'You mean –'

'What else do spiders do with their prey, Tansy? They don't keep it to look at, you know!'

'Can you help him?'

Flissy grinned. 'Of course. Spider venom's fairly easy – even from a spider the size of Spiderwitch!' She busied herself with dried herbs, hot water and honey, and fairly rapidly Taliesin, weak and watery, was back with us.

'How on earth did you get yourself caught, Taliesin?' Gwydion wanted to know. 'Last time we saw you, in Cantre'r Gwaelod, you were on your way to Merlin – straight back, you said, Merlin needed you, you said!'

Taliesin eased himself into a sitting position. 'I

allowed myself to get side-tracked. I wanted to take a look at Ynys Haf for myself, see what the situation was, so I could report to Merlin. Then I saw someone familiar disappear into a cave halfway up a mountain, and I couldn't believe my eyes. So I followed her. Unfortunately, she'd spotted me, too. She was waiting for me. She had me before I could protect myself, and the last thing I remember is a very large pair of spider fangs closing on my shoulder.' He rubbed it, ruefully. 'Thanks for rescuing me, you two. I didn't much fancy being a spider's lunch.'

'So what now?' I asked, my lips feeling a bit stiff-upper-ish. 'Are you heading back to Camelot and Merlin?' I desperately wanted his kindness, his support, his help.

5

'Half a mo',' Taliesin said, shutting his eyes and concentrating. He opened them again. 'Damnation. He's switched off his aura again. That means I'm going to have to go and fetch him.'

'Fetch who?' I asked, stupidly.

'Merlin, of course. What's happening in Ynys Haf is much too serious for him to be gadding about elsewhere in Time. Arthur and Guinevere will just have to sort themselves out.' He snorted. 'Guinevere! I ask you! What was wrong with Gwenhwyfar? Perfectly good Welsh name, but no, she had to go and change it. Typical! Yes. The Matter of Britain can wait a while. Ynys Haf is much more important.'

'You're absolutely right, Taliesin,' Flissy agreed, 'Merlin *should* be here. Tansy and Gwydion can sort out Spiderwitch and rescue T.A. and Elffin and all the rest of it, but Ynys Haf is Merlin's responsibility, and he should be here right now.'

I still couldn't get my head round Merlin not caring two hoots about the people of Ynys Haf. It seemed so callous, somehow. But I suppose it's the way he is. He knows that people will go on whatever happens, it's human nature to survive, but Ynys Haf must be protected, and Merlin is responsible for it.

'Anyway,' Taliesin said, getting groggily to his feet and stretching his bruised shoulder. 'I suppose I'd better make myself scarce. I need to get Merlin back here as soon as I can, so that he can sort out Ynys Haf's problems.'

'Oh, no you don't,' Flissy said firmly, 'you aren't going anywhere until you've eaten and rested. You certainly aren't going gadding about in Time AND space without a good, hot meal. So you just go up onto the sleeping loft and get a few hours' sleep while I make a nice stew to keep you going. Put some meat on those ribs of yours! You haven't been eating properly, have you?'

Taliesin hid a grin behind his hand, but obediently climbed the ladder to the platform to rest.

'That's such a relief,' sighed Gwydion, wandering to the back door, and looking out at the rows of vegetables wilting in the dry earth. 'Merlin can sort this out, and we can do the rest of it.'

I was still feeling mutinous. 'Oh, great. We get to tackle Spiderwitch, and Conor of the Land Beneath, and rescue T.A. and Elffin. Always assuming Conor's leprechaun army isn't already on its way right this minute because the fake Maebh has reverted to a heap of straw and mud!'

'We can do it, Tanz. We have to. If Merlin's coming back, we can head for Erin and forget about Spiderwitch for a bit. Once Ynys Haf is fixed, Merlin won't let her get out of hand again – he'll at least contain her until we get back to sort her out.'

'Oh, goody, goody!' I said sarcastically. 'Can't wait!'

Taliesin, rested and fed and now a barn owl, took off into the night sky, his silvery-white wings ghostly in the moonlight. His blood-curdling screech drifted back on the warm night air. Once he reached a Time Door, he could go back to Camelot and fetch Merlin.

Now for our mission. Next morning Branwen, Flissy and Nest stood in the doorway of the *tŷ hir* and waved us off, two black-backed gulls heading towards the coast, to meet up first with Gwyddno Garanhir at Cantre'r Gwaelod. He had assembled an army, and it was marching importantly up and down his castle courtyard, drilled by a square, bossy man with white hair that stuck up in a bristle cut to look like a hedgehog. Gwyddno was in his solar, poring over maps and worrying his wife to bits. She was frantic anyway because of Elffin, and Gwyddno wasn't helping, being in Prepare for Bloody Battle mode rather than Reassure the Little Woman mode.

'For goodness sake woman, don't fuss!' he bellowed as we entered the solar. Lady G dabbed her eyes and sniffled. 'The boy will be fine, I tell you! He's bright and he's brave, and no four-foot Irish fairy is going to get the better of him!'

I had a quiet grin, hearing Conor of the Land Beneath described as a four-foot fairy: good thing he couldn't hear! At least, I hoped he couldn't. I hoped there weren't any of his spies in Gwyddno's court . . .

'It's all that human girl's fault!' Lady Garanhir wailed. 'She flirted with him and turned his head, and he forgot all about that nice princess he's been betrothed to since he was six!'

'Ridiculous age to betroth anybody,' Gwyddno muttered. 'And a bit of flirting never did any harm, not ever. Now pull yourself together, my love. I can't be doing with all this weeping and wailing.'

He turned, and saw Gwydion and me. 'Oh, it's you

two, is it?' he muttered. 'About time, too. My men are champing at the bit to get over the water and have a go at them foreigners!'

Gwydion sat down opposite Gwyddno, whose face was more distracted and grumpy than I'd ever seen it. No matter what he said to his wife, Gwyddno Garanhir was very, very worried about his son.

'I don't think it's a good idea to go over there with an army, Gwyddno,' said Gwydion tentatively. 'I think a stealthy approach would make more sense. Find out what the situation is, decide how best to tackle it, and then, if we need to, bring in your fighting men.'

Gwyddno scowled. 'Stealthy approach?' he roared. 'The only approach these people understand is a jolly good wallop with a longsword around their beastly ears!'

Gwydion breathed deeply and spoke slowly, deliberately. 'But if we can avoid bloodshed on *both* sides, Gwyddno, and rescue them anyway, wouldn't that be altogether better?'

'Humph. And how do you propose to do that?'

'First,' Gwydion said, 'we get over there, and find T.A. and Elffin. Then, if they are rescuable, we rescue them. If they aren't, we try diplomacy, and as a very last resort, we'll get tough.'

Gwyddno Garanhir opened his mouth to protest, but then the door opened and a familiar figure waltzed in. Maebh. *Still as gorgeously pretty as ever*, I thought disgustedly.

'Oh, Dragonking dear!' she dimpled, and dropped a mocking little curtsy. 'Wasn't I just the minute wondering when you'd be back!'

Gwydion smiled with his teeth, but not his eyes. 'Were you? Are you well?'

'Oh, I'm well enough, I am so,' she twittered, twirling round and making her frilly pink skirt fly out, 'but I'm terrible bored. There's not a thing at all to do here in this place, there is not!'

'Really?' Gwydion murmured uninterestedly, and turned back to Gwyddno Garanhir. 'So, my Lord. Are we agreed?'

'Agreed? Oh, and what might it be that you've agreed, Gwyddno Garanhir?' Maebh trilled. 'Something altogether exciting, I'll be bound!'

'That we're not sending my –'

'– Aunt Flissy a basket of jellied eels,' I interrupted, scowling at the Lord of Cantre'r Gwaelod. 'Are we, Gwyd?'

'Absolutely not,' he replied solemnly. 'Smoked salmon or nothing!'

'Oh, you're teasing, you are so!' Maebh tittered. She knew something was up, she just didn't know what.

It had done the trick, though. Gwyddno put a guard on his tongue, and our plans were concluded away from Maebh's dainty lug-holes.

I once solemnly swore that I would never again get on anything that floats. Well, now was crunch time. Gwyddno wouldn't have had strong enough wings to fly right across the Irish Sea, having never shape-shifted before, and so – yes, you guessed. Boat.

It seemed churlish to fly solo when everyone else was spanking along in a boat, and there was also a high wind that made flying difficult anyway. So, reluctantly, I climbed aboard.

By the time the coast of Ireland hove in sight, I had stopped being sea-sick. I didn't have anything left to be sick with.

Once we were on shore we shifted Gwyddno, since he should be more or less safe overland. Once he'd got the hang of flying he took to it like a – well, like a bird, I suppose. He was thoroughly enjoying being a rook, tumbling round the sky croaking hoarsely with delight. We flapped over the cottage on the shore where Big Deirdre, the size-shifting giantess, lived. It nestled back against the hill, a goat contentedly cropping the thatched roof, but there was no sign of the large lady herself, which was just as well, because I didn't have the energy to cope with her right then.

We decided, especially since I still felt wobbly, to rest before tackling Conor. We found a sheltered spot on the side of a hill, and shifted Gwyddno back. It took him a while to get out of the rook-type strut, but he eventually settled down to helping Gwydion build a shelter for the night out of some branches and bracken. Then they built a fire and I magicked some decent food. Did I mention I'm trying to wean myself off junk food? Well, I am. I decided, if I'm going to college, I'm going to have to learn to eat vegetables and yuk stuff like that to keep myself healthy. Mam does it at the moment, makes me eat my greens and so on, but hey, I'm a big girl now. Time I did it for myself, right?

So it was steak and kidney pie and runner beans and buttery mashed potatoes and fresh fruit salad for afters. Gwyddno Garanhir, having never tasted pineapple, peach, mango or kiwi before was highly impressed, but he was a bit dubious about the mashed potato.

'You really eat this stuff in your Time?' he said, squishing it with his knife. 'I can hardly believe something as bland as this will catch on!'

'It isn't always bland,' I pointed out. 'Sometimes it's chips. You should ask O'Liam about that!'

He couldn't, right then, of course. O'Liam of the Green Boots was making up for lost time with Siobhan Flowerface, his bride-to-be, and we'd left him behind. He had about two hundred years of courting to do before his wedding day. I hoped we'd be back for that, with T.A. and Elffin safe and sound. I do like a nice wedding!

We slept undisturbed, and I woke to a glorious sunrise, birds shrieking in every bush and tree, and the equally glorious smell of frying bacon, eggs, mushrooms, fried bread, grilled tomato and sausages. Gwyddno approved of a full Welsh Breakfast, even though that hadn't been invented yet either. In fact he approved so much that we had a bit of difficulty getting him airborne afterwards!

I couldn't eat much: I had a sinking, sick feeling when I thought of the day to come. Last time I'd been here, I'd decided that if I never, ever saw Conor of the Land Beneath again, it would be much too soon. But here I was again, heading for Conor's Kingdom under the earth.

I tried not to think about what the day held in store. It would come soon enough.

6

I half expected to see hordes of warlike leprechauns marching up and down, and maybe bits of fake Maebh scattered all over the place, but when we reached the entrance to the Land Beneath, all was quiet.

Too quiet. There was something about it that made my antennae twitch. And yes, I did have antennae. Ants do, you know. We sneaked under the door into Conor's kingdom, and scrambled quickly down the corridor to his council chamber.

We went past the two lumpish sentries guarding it without them noticing us. One of them was actually snoring! Inside was heaving with activity. Robed leprechauns were bustling about with piles of documents under their arms, several were sitting at high desks scribbling away furiously, but there was no sign of Conor or his prisoners.

'Wonder where His Nibs is?' I muttered, but Gwydion was already heading back to the door. Outside, we huddled against the wall so that we wouldn't accidentally get stepped on by a scurrying leprechaun secretary (Lepretary? Secrechaun?).

'If we concentrate really hard,' Gwydion suggested, twitching his feelers, 'we might be able to pick him up.'

So, six-legged radio receivers, we concentrated, and after a couple of minutes of running a little way in one direction, and then in another, we finally picked up a feeling of Conor – but couldn't find a trace of T.A. or Elffin at all.

'Right,' Gwydion said determinedly, 'there's Conor. If we can find him, perhaps he'll let slip where the others are.'

So we headed where the Conor-sense was leading us. He was in a luxurious bedchamber. Did I say luxurious! It was *opulent*! It had a huge four-poster bed with a roof and those draped curtain thingies in gold lamé fabric, thick tapestries on the walls and floor, and even a window to the outside. At least, I thought it was a window until I got a proper look. It was actually just painted on the wall – a scene with a river and trees and stuff, very lifelike. *Trompe l'oeil*, it's called. (You know, when they paint something on a wall to make it look as if something real is there when it isn't. Impressed? So you ought to be. I know posh words, *and* I use them occasionally!)

But the bed was real enough, and Conor of the Land Beneath was on a chair beside it, holding the hand of someone lying flat on their back. I couldn't tell who from down there on the floor.

Gwydion climbed up the gold fringing dangling off the bed, until he was high enough to see, then back down again. His ant-y face was amazed.

'It's the fake-Maebh!' he whispered. 'She's still in one piece, although it looks as though her battery has gone flat.'

'She hasn't got a battery, Gwyd,' I pointed out. Gwyddno Garanhir was staring from one to the other of us, bemused.

'What are you talking about?' he demanded.

'We made a fake Maebh so that we could get O'Liam and Siobhan away without giving him the real one. She looks perfect, but she didn't have much in the way of conversation. She smiled a lot. She was good enough to fool Conor, though.'

Gwyddno Garanhir looked even more confused. 'Fake? How can you make a fake person?'

'It's a long story,' I whispered, 'but at the moment it looks like the magic is holding up, which is more than I expected. So we may have a bit of time to find T.A. and Elffin before she crumbles away.'

'C-crumbles away?' Gwyddno stammered, nervously.

'I'll explain later,' I muttered, and set off for the door of the chamber.

Outside, we got in a huddle to discuss the situation. 'Fake Maebh might be holding up,' Gwydion said, 'but it looks as if Conor is worried about her. I still can't sense any trace of the others.'

I sent out my instincts and listened, but Gwydion was right. Wherever they were, they were either shielded in some way, or they weren't in the Land Beneath at all. The trouble was, if they were elsewhere, where would we even begin to look?

'I think we should search here before we start haring off madly in all directions,' I decided at last. 'If we do that, then at least we're sure where they aren't.'

'That'll be a help,' Gwydion said, sarcastically.

'Got any better ideas, smartypants?' I enquired. 'No? Right then. Start looking.'

We scuttled up and down corridors on our little ant feet, waving our antennae madly trying to pick up T.A. and Elffin. We went in and out of ballrooms, storerooms, kitchens, living rooms, you name it, we visited it. We even found Conor of the Land Beneath's

Trophy Room, and *that* made us stop and think, I can tell you. Remember Big Deirdre, who was really upset at Conor because he'd killed her cub? Well, we found Deirdre's beamish boy, or rather, a bit of him. His head was mounted on a wooden shield fastened to the wall. And his wasn't the only trophy head, either. There were a couple of Tylwyth Teg (like Nest!), a goblin, a troll, several baby dragons, a unicorn and a hippogriff. It was horrible, and made me even more determined to make Conor of the Land Beneath pay for his evilness somehow. I even found myself feeling sorry for Big Deirdre. If my baby son's head had been chopped off, stuffed and mounted on a wooden shield, I'd probably be a bit upset, too!

Feeling rather sick, I led the way outside, and down the corridor. We came to another door. It had roses round the entrance, and I suddenly recognsed O'Liam's Old Mammy's room. We scuttled underneath the door and there she was, Brigid of the Light Fingers.

The old lady sat crocheting something lacy, rocking back and forth in her chair as if butter wouldn't melt – when actually it would probably sizzle and turn brown. I thought for a second or two, and then shape-shifted back into me. I did it slowly, so that she'd see me coming from the feet up. The last thing I wanted was to scare the old dear – she might have a heart-attack and die if I suddenly whizzed into me without any warning!

I was fooling myself. She hardly looked up.

'Is it yourself, Lady?' she said calmly. 'Is yer man there also?'

Gwydion shimmered into shape beside me, and then shifted Gwyddno Garanhir. Both men had to bend their heads so they wouldn't collide with the ceiling.

Her eyes sparkled. 'Ah, and isn't it a fine figure of a man!' she said happily, putting down her crochet. 'And who might this other young fellow be?'

Gwydion introduced Gwyddno Garanhir, who was highly amused to be called a 'young fellow'. Her eyes widened with recognition. 'Ah, is that who you are? Didn't I once go on a day trip to your place when I was a wee girl? All the way there across the Middlesome Sea and all the way back on a boat, and lunch on your fine big wall half way.'

Gwyddno preened. He was proud of his wall.

'All the same,' Brigid continued, 'you want to make sure you close them big old gates when the great tides are upon you, or you'll be up to your necks and your noses in sea-water, so you will.'

I couldn't have put it better myself!

Gwyddno cleared his throat. 'Ahem, madam, dear lady, you needn't worry on that account. My gatekeeper is entirely conscientious.'

And a drunk, I thought, miserably, *who is going to drink himself silly in a sulk because you're having a party and he isn't invited. And then – goodbye Cantre'r Gwaelod!*

Still, no time to worry about that now. Cantre'r Gwaelod was perfectly safe while Gwyddno and Elffin weren't there.

'What can I be doing for youse?' Brigid enquired, getting up and walking round Gwydion as if he were a statue in a museum. I kept a close eye on her hands – she was the best pickpocket in the world.

'We're looking for my friend, T.A.,' I explained. 'She's with Gwyddno Garanhir's son, Elffin. We thought that Conor had captured them, but we can't find them anywhere here.'

'Well, you wouldn't, would you, so?'

'Why would that be?' Gwydion asked patiently, knowing there was no hurrying the old dear.

'They aren't here at all, not a wart nor a whisker of them, no not at all.'

'Do you know where they are?' I asked.

'I do, so.' She sat down again and picked up her crochet.

'Can you tell us where?'

'I can, so. The question is, will I?'

Gwydion turned on the charm. It works, sometimes. He dropped to one knee so that his face was only a foot or two above her little wizened mischievous one. 'Will you help us, Brigid of the Light Fingers? For the sake of our friendship with your son O'Liam? Please?'

She contemplated him like a bright-eyed little bird. 'Ah, if you put it like that, Gwydion Dragonking, and for the sake of O'Liam my son, yes, I will tell you.'

Gwydion, Gwyddno and I waited.

'And?' Gwydion prompted.

'They are where sunlight shines on a fine morning, but where darkness rules all day. They are within sound of bells, and neither up nor down.'

'Thanks a bunch,' I muttered.

'Not at all, not at all,' Brigid smiled. 'Will that be it, now?'

'Can't you be a bit more specific?' I asked, patiently.

'I could. But I won't. You young people are all the same. Impatient, impatient, won't use the brains *Dia uilechumhachtach* Himself gave you. Now, be off. It's time for my nap.'

Fairly obviously, we weren't going to get any more help here.

'There's one other wee thing you might need,' Brigid added, just as we fizzed down into ants again. We waited.

'The silver key that Conor keeps close,' she said casually.

I shifted back to me again. 'A silver key? Why do we need that? What does it unlock?'

'You'll find out, I dare say. When you've a need to.'

Thanks a bunch, O'Liam's Mammy! Not.

Outside, and ants again, we went into a huddle.

'So,' Gwydion mused. 'Where it's sunny in the morning but dark all day, within sound of bells, and neither up nor down. Maybe we could go and ask the Hermit of Glendalough. If he's awake and Padraig will let us see him.'

'Wave a bacon butty at Padraig and he'd probably *give* you the Hermit, never mind let you see him,' I said. 'But I don't see how the hermit could help us this time, Gwyd. O.K., he told us more or less where to find you but he didn't exactly give us a route map.'

'Perhaps if we start at the beginning, try to work out what the sunlight in the morning part means,' Gwyddno suggested.

'It might be better,' I said, thinking fast, 'if we

could work out the sound of bells bit. If we can hear bells, we can head in that direction and see if anything else around also fits the bill.'

But first, of course, we had to find the silver key in Conor's chamber.

7

We knew we'd been in Conor's chamber somewhere along the line, but there were dozens and dozens of rooms in the Land Beneath, and we couldn't remember exactly where it was. So it was a while before we found it again. All we had to do was get inside, get the silver key and get out again, right?

The problem was, Conor was now inside. He'd abandoned the fake Maebh – well, maybe her conversation was a bit lacking! His own room was just as posh as Maebh's, but not exactly the décor I'd have chosen.

The walls were lined with dark red satiny stuff, there were dark red carpets on the floor, crimson candles burned on every flat surface and in dozens of candlesticks and wall-brackets too. A huge fire roared in the hearth, the smoke disappearing up a coppery flue-thing that snaked along the walls and up through the ceiling. The whole room had a reddish glow, and what with the fire and the candles, the temperature was like a sauna. Conor didn't seem to notice it, though. He slumped, his chin resting on his hand, in a high-backed, throne-type chair beside the fire. His huge four-poster bed stood with its head against the wall, with a table at the side and a carved wooden chest along the foot.

I had a quick look round to try and spot the key, but couldn't see it anywhere. Gwydion climbed up the leg of the bedside table to see if it was there, and Gwyddno checked out the top of the chest, but no luck. We were in a huddle deciding where to look next when Conor stood up and stretched. Something chinkled. A bunch of keys was attached to his belt.

I nudged Gwydion. 'Look!' I whispered.

He groaned. 'How on earth are we supposed to get those when he's wearing the damn things?'

'Maybe Brigid the Light Fingered might –?' I suggested.

Gwydion shook his head. 'I doubt it. She'd tell us to use our initiative. I don't think she'll help us any more than she already has. These are her people, this is her king, don't forget. If she helps us too much, she'd feel guilty, I expect.'

I gave him an old-fashioned look. 'I don't think the Land Beneath's Chief Pickpocket feels very guilty about anything, Gwyd!'

'All the same, I don't think she'll help us. Maybe if O'Liam was with us . . .'

'Even leprechaun kings sleep some time,' Gwyddno said. 'I doubt if he'll get in bed with all his clothes on. He's bound to take his belt off, then, at least.'

'So all we have to do is wait,' I said, not having thought of that.

So we waited. And waited. And waited. Waited while Conor of the Land Beneath ate his supper (very large and consisting of large quantities of rabbit stew, fruit pies, and sticky sweetmeats). Waited while Conor brushed his teeth (just as well after all those sweeties). Then he was undressed and helped into his nightshirt (I closed my eyes for that bit, don't worry!) by his servant-leprechauns. His hair was tucked under a frilly nightcap thing, and the leprechaun king was tucked up into his four-poster bed, snuggled down among several large, fluffy pillows. The cords holding back the red satin bed-hangings were untied, but before the curtains were drawn across (what for? To keep out the draughts? Good grief!) an ancient lady leprechaun came in and drew up a chair beside the bed. She was so old she could have been the Glendalough Hermit's Mam!

She sat down, and from her vast carpet-bag she produced a book, opened it – and read Conor a bed-time story.

Conor, whose great golden eyes never left the old woman's crumpled, ancient face, grew drowsier and drowsier as she read him a tale of a beautiful leprechaun princess and a handsome leprechaun King (naturally, called Conor). True Love conquered all, as it invariably does in fairy stories, and by the time she'd said, 'and they all lived happily ever after, they did so,' Conor of the Land Beneath was snuggled down beneath the coverlet.

'Night night, Conor. Sleep tight. Don't let the bugs bite now,' the old lady whispered, kissing the leprechaun king on the forehead.

'Nighty-night, nanny,' Conor muttered sleepily, 'the bugs will not get me at all, I promise,' and almost before she had left the room was fast asleep and snoring contentedly.

The clothes he'd taken off had been neatly folded into the chest, but the bunch of keys rested on the table beside the bed. Now, all we had to do was get hold of the right key, and then – we were out of there!

When we were sure that Conor was sound asleep,

Gwydion shifted beside the table, and slowly closed his hand over the bunch of keys. He tried to gather them up silently, then, carrying the bunch of keys, he crossed the chamber and carefully opened the door. Gwyddno and I scuttled out, and waited impatiently (still ants) while Gwydion sorted through the keys, looking for a silver one. There were three.

'Which one is it, Tanz?' he whispered.

'How am I supposed to know?'

'What am I going to do? How can I tell?'

'You can't, dingbat. Take them all!'

'He'll notice if I take all three.'

'Not if I magic some replicas, he won't.'

So I shifted back to me, and magicked three identical silver keys. We took the real ones, of course – I didn't want to risk taking the fakes in case there was some sort of a spell on the real ones. You can never tell, with keys.

Then, of course, Gwydion had to return the keys to Conor's bedside table.

He dropped them.

They hit the floor with an almighty jangle that would have woken the dead if there had been any lying about. Conor sat bolt upright, his great, dark-lashed eyes jerking open, his golden hair standing on end where the pillows had mussed it.

Fortunately Gwydion thinks fast on his feet – as the keys began their descent, so did Gwydion, phutting down into an ant so fast that the air made a weird noise, as if someone had stuck a finger in their cheek and popped it.

Conor looked sleepily around him, confused,

wondering what had woken him. Then his eyes lit on the bunch of keys on the floor beside the bed. He threw back his covers, slid out of bed and picked them up. Looked carefully at them. Counted them (and counted them on his fingers, as well! Obviously numbers were as much a problem as letters). Satisfied, he got back into bed, although he looked suspiciously around the chamber first, peering behind the bed-hangings and the tapestries to make sure no one was hiding there. When he lay down again, the keys were under his pillow.

Didn't matter. We had the three we needed. All we had to do was find the right key, and the lock that it fitted.

Of course, three little ants can't actually carry three keys. So I turned each one into a grass seed and we each carried one on the long journey out of the Land Beneath.

Once we were well away from the entrance, we shifted again, this time into a trio of long-eared owls, each carrying a silver key, our slight bodies silhouetted against a huge amber moon. We could have gone in any direction – after all, we didn't have a clue where we were supposed to go – but we headed west, almost by instinct. The moon was fading against the dawn sky when we glided silently down to the base of a tree, shifted, and thought about breakfast. I spat the key out of my mouth and Gwydion and Gwyddno followed suit.

Three keys gleamed on the palm of my hand. They were almost identical: silver, about four inches long, only slight variations in the knobbly end. Each one had that faint tingle about it that betrayed the presence of magic . . . No clues otherwise, however. We'd just have to wait until we found a lock to try.

We ate breakfast and rested for a couple of hours, getting our strength back. We lay in the sunshine, drowsing, but all the time keeping part of our senses alert for danger. We dared not forget for an instant that we were in a foreign land full of some very scary creatures, if O'Liam of the Green Boots could be believed. Pwca horses, the Great Worm of Mullingar, the Terrible Beast of Loch Ree – what had been the others? Oh, yes, the Black Dog of Tullamore and the Howling Spirits of Armagh. It would probably be a good idea to keep our eyes open.

Late in the afternoon, we moved on, still flying south, all three of us feeling instinctively that that was the right direction to travel in. We were kestrels, our long, rakish wings and dark-barred tails cutting through the late afternoon sky with shallow beats of our wings, the red of the setting sun painting the countryside mellow amber below us.

As night fell, we glided one after another into an ancient yew tree alongside a tiny, even more ancient, church. Built of stone, it had only one set of plain, greenish, thick-glassed windows and a wobbly-looking tower. The yew was shelter for the night, so we roosted and slept. None of us was hungry. As light faded, the stars came out, speckling the unclouded heavens with bright pinpoints of brilliance, and the Lady Moon sailed serenely overhead. I was comforted by Her presence and slept soundly.

Doooonnnnggg! Dooooonnnnggg! Dooooonnnnggg!

I fell off my perch, recovering myself halfway down, squawking with terror, back-pedalling frantically on thin air before I hit the ground. Gwydion jumped almost out of his feathers and staggered backwards, only just managing to hang on with his talons, lunge with his hooked beak and grab Gwyddno's tail-feathers to stop him falling off his perch.

Safely back in the tree, I fanned myself with my wing, still shaking at my narrow escape. The tiny moustaches over Gwydion and Gwyddno's beaks gave them a piratical air, but they were just as shaken as I was.

'Phew!' I squawked, and the bell bonged on, the rickety little church tower reverberating with the noise.

Over the hill and along the road came a column of people in their Sunday best tunics and dresses, summoned to the church by the clangour, in ones, twos, threes and more, whole families. Into the church they went, one after another, and at last the bell stopped clanging. My bird-brain was trying to remember something, but it wasn't quite big enough to grasp whatever it was. I flew down a few feet to a solid branch, shimmered and shifted into girl form, hanging on tightly and taking great care not to look down in case I got dizzy. Then I put my human brain to work.

Sound of a bell! Of course! I shifted again and flew back up to the others. Slow, or what?

'It's a bell, guys!' I squeaked excitedly. 'Remember what Brigid said? "Within sound of bells", she said!'

'So she did,' Gwydion said thoughtfully. 'Bells. Not just one. Bells, not bell.'

Then, in the distance, we heard a second bell begin tolling, and a third, and another and another – in every small surrounding village there seemed to be a church or a chapel, and every single one seemed to have a bell!

'Blooming bells everywhere,' Gwydion said mournfully. 'I suppose we'd better start looking for the rest of it! The morning sun and the daytime dark and all that stuff.'

For nearly half the day we flapped around uselessly. There were churches with bonging bells every-flipping-where! This part of Ireland seemed to have cornered the market in bells! We quit around lunch-time. Our tummies were rumbling, and even though there was plenty of food around that rooks would have really enjoyed, I fancied something a bit more solid.

Gwyddno was mightily impressed by fried chicken. Yes, all right, I know I said I was trying to wean myself off junk food, but I'm allowed a moment of weakness every now and again, aren't I? *And* I had chips as well, wanna make an issue of it? It had been a frustrating morning. Then I magicked some blackberry tart and cream, then some Pantysgawn cheese and crackers, so that was healthy, wasn't it? Gwyddno chomped into the cheese as if he'd never tasted cheese before – but then, he'd never tasted Pantysgawn, and if you like smelly, white, squishy, delicious cheese, that's the one for you.

While we munched, we chucked ideas around.

'If it's sunlight on a fine morning,' I suggested, dunking a chip in ketchup, 'then it has to be east-facing, right? Sun rises in the east and sinks in the west and all that.'

'I suppose so. But then,' Gwydion picked up another piece of fried chicken from the red-and-white striped bucket, 'if darkness rules all day, that means it's somewhere where there will be deep shadow as soon as the sun has risen, and if it's east facing, that doesn't make sense.'

'Unless,' Gwyddno mumbled through a handful of chips, 'the sun goes up and over wherever it is and leaves it in darkness.'

'Like a cave in a cliff or something?' I said.

'Or a mountain.'

'That's it!' I spluttered, choking on a blackberry, '*that's* what it reminded me of. The Grand Old Duke of York!'

'Pardon?' Gwydion and Gwyddno looked at me, totally mystified, never having been bounced on their Mam-gu's knee to a nursery rhyme when they were little. At least, not to that nursery rhyme!

'The Grand Old Duke of York,' I sang, 'he had ten thousand men. He marched them up to the top of the hill and he marched them down again.'

'Thanks, Tanz,' Gwydion muttered, pinching a lump of my pie, 'that's really helpful.'

'I haven't finished,' I said, pinching it back again, 'the pie or the song. And when they were up they were up, and when they were down they were down, and when they were only half way up – *they were neither up nor down!*'

They both stared at me. 'I think I see what you're getting at,' Gwydion said slowly. 'So, we need a place halfway up the side of a hill, perhaps a cave or something, that's sunny in the morning, and dark all day!'

'Exactly!' I crowed, triumphantly.

I was wrong, of course. That was much too easy. When we'd eaten and cleared away the wrappers and bones and stuff we lay around for a while letting our lunch go down. Once we'd stopped burping and groaning we shifted into rooks again and flapped west, following the sun, looking for a hill.

Well of course, there were plenty of those, but we couldn't find one with a cave half way up its eastern side. They all had eastern sides, naturally, but not one of them had a cave that we could see. It was almost dark when we found it.

Now, you probably know me quite well by now, so you'll know that my Chief Talent is Cowardice. With a capital Cow. And when we found this place, all my Cowardice stood up on end and waved its arms. 'Help,' it screamed, 'get me out of here!'

It was a castle, halfway up the east-facing slope of a bare, rock-strewn mountainside. And I could tell just by looking at it that it wasn't a nice homely, friendly castle. The black-washed stone walls told me that. It had been painted so black that it seemed to swallow light, so black that it was almost a shadow itself, so black that it was more than just black, it was a total absence of light. The vultures perching on the towers didn't help, either, or the tiny, sinister arrow-slits, and the skeletons in the cages dangling from the walls and the grinning skulls ornamenting the battlements. All of them emphasised and underlined that this was a Nasty, Scary Castle, Grade I, Gold Star with Knobs On. The sinking sun tried to dye the western side of it red, but it couldn't manage more than a reddish black. Who, or what, would live in a place as black as this?

One thing was certain. It was most definitely the place where Conor of the Land Beneath had put T.A. and Elffin. I could feel them.

'There is no way I am going in there tonight,' I said through gritted beak. 'No way, nohow, not at all.'

'Nor me,' Gwydion agreed.

'I wish I'd brought my army,' Gwyddno said darkly. 'I'd have that place pulled to a pile of black rubble in no time. I'd find my boy and T.A. if I had to take it apart stone by stone, yes I would indeed.'

'What about the people inside?' Gwydion asked. 'And how many of them? And how fierce? And what do they have in the way of weapons?'

'All the same,' Gwyddno said. 'I wish I'd brought my army.'

I could relate to that, no problem. I wished he'd brought his army, too. Then I could have gone home and left the battle to him.

'Tomorrow,' I said, making an executive decision and flapping off in the general direction of away-from-the-castle. 'We'll tackle it tomorrow.' The further away I was that night, the happier I'd be. 'Tomorrow, in nice, bright daylight, we'll come back and get inside and see who's in there. If we can find T.A. and Elffin and shift them, maybe we can be in and out in no time, and home in half that again. Perhaps.'

'Except for the key,' Gwydion reminded me as we glided in to land. 'Somewhere along the line we have to use the silver key. Brigid of the Light Fingers told us so.'

'Maybe she was lying,' I suggested. 'Leprechauns do, you know. They're well known for their sneakiness.' Underneath, of course, I knew perfectly well that it wouldn't be as easy as that. Never is, is it? Not for me, anyway.

The sun slanting through the trees woke us next morning, shining directly into our eyes. We breakfasted quickly, shifted into starlings and headed for the castle, leaving the three silver keys tucked safely into a squirrel's drey. My iridescent summer plumage glinted in the sunshine, and my poached eggs on toast roiled in my innards. I wished I hadn't bothered with breakfast, because I thought I might be sick. Gruesome skeletons in cages dangling off walls tend to do that to a person, I find.

Sure enough, the castle was bathed in brilliant morning sunshine. It didn't make it look any less sinister, only sinisterly sunlit. Dew-drop diamonds twinkled on the bleached bones dangling in the rusty cages (iron cages – extra scary for a witch!). It flashed cheerily on skulls and grinning choppers and glimmered sunnily through empty eye sockets in a horribly disconcerting way, and I wished I was somewhere – anywhere – else. Apart from these points of relative (and inappropriate) brightness (I mean, how bright can a bone twinkle?) the Castle was black as the inside of a bat's pyjamas.

We perched in a tree, and I settled in between Gwydion and Gwyddno for safety.

'That,' Gwydion squawked, 'is one scary castle.'

'Thanks, Gwyd,' I muttered. 'State the obvious, why don't you?'

'Once we're inside, it won't be so bad, because we'll actually be doing something positive,' he said. If we can find T.A. and Elffin, we can come back and get the keys when we find out what we need them for. Or the one key we need, anyway.'

'Inside, then,' I said miserably. 'All right. Come on.'
And I *led the way* . . .

What am I? Stupid or something? Don't answer that, please, it wouldn't be polite.

I flipped through a narrow arrow slit in a round tower and into a room that, apart from a thin band of light where the sun risked coming inside, was completely dark. I wondered if we might be better off being owls, and then had an even better idea, and shifted into a whiskered bat, which, since it flies during the day sometimes, would be equally good in the dark or in the light. Our radar would also keep us from flying into walls and stuff. Gwydion saw the sense of this and shifted himself and Gwyddno too.

The room we were in was empty except for a wooden bench, but the door stood open so at least we could get out. One by one we flitted out into a passageway, curved to the tower walls. We flew high, up above eye-level, so that anyone coming round the bend wouldn't see us. Even as bats we wanted to be as unobtrusive as possible. The place seemed completely empty. There was none of the hustle and bustle that energised Castell Du and Castell y Ddraig. It was silent as the grave – no, not a good thought at all, Tanz. Silent as a soggy Sunday in Sarnau. That's better.

There was also a most peculiar and unpleasant *smell* about the place. Dampness, mould, and something else I couldn't identify. It made me feel oddly panicky. I ask you, a smell, making me feel oomphy diddlum, as my Mam-gu used to call it.

We flitted and flapped from empty chamber to

empty passageway, from empty tower to empty tower. We scoured that castle from attic to dungeon (T.A. and Elffin weren't in there, thank goodness) and it was completely devoid of human life.

Frustrated and puzzled, we ended up in the attic among dust-covered boxes and chests. I found a beam, folded my leathery wings and dangled upside down.

'I'm going to have one more look, see if there's anything we've missed,' Gwydion squeaked.

'I'll come with you,' Gwyddno squeaked back. 'They have to be here somewhere.'

I clenched my batty toenails and closed my eyes to try to catch a bit of a batnap. Suddenly a voice in my ear made me jump.

'Hello, gorgeous!' it said.

Pardon? I swivelled my head sideways. Dangling upside down beside me was a gentleman bat. He had an amazing set of whiskers – I almost expected him to start twiddling them like a Victorian villain.

'Oh, puh-lease!' I replied, far too tired to put up with someone – even a bat – trying to chat me up. 'Get lost, why don't you?'

'Aha, me proud beauty,' my admirer squeaked, sidling closer upside-down. 'Don't spurn me, now, will you! I've been waiting all my life for such as you! Marry me, *mo chridh*, and have my bat-babies!'

'I'd rather poke myself in the eye with a sharp stick,' I said crossly. 'Buzz off.'

'Ha! Bats don't buzz.' He edged closer, until he could reach out his leather wing and stroke my ears. 'Give us a kiss?'

'Oh, good grief,' I muttered, and resisted the

temptation to turn into something large and bat-eating. 'Look, I'm not interested, all right? I've had a very bad day, and I'm really in no mood for this. So make like snow and melt away, all right?'

'Tell me about your day,' he said silkily, snuggling closer. 'I'm a gooood listener!'

'You want to know about my day?' I asked crossly. 'All right, I'll tell you. It started much too early this morning, and I've spent the whole day looking for a sign of life – any sign of life – in this horrible castle.'

'Well, you'll not find that here at all, will you?' my suitor squeaked. 'Sure, and you'd hardly expect it here, not where everybody's altogether dead! Isn't that what the Black Castle of Ballygar is all about?'

Now that startled me so much I forgot to clench my toenails and I promptly fell off my beam.

8

'Now let me get this straight,' I said, fluttering my way back up, 'you say everybody here is dead?'

'Deceased As Dead Doornails, they are so,' he said with a twitch of his whiskers.

'So they're ghosts, right? So why can't I see them?'

He looked at me pityingly. 'You'd not see ghosts unless they want you to see them, now would you? Isn't that the whole idea?'

'I don't know, do I? I've never met a ghost.' I looked around, nervously. 'How do I know where they are?'

'Well, you don't, at all, isn't that the way of it? Besides, you're even less likely to see them than a human would. Humans see them remarkable well, because they're just so afraid of them. Your ghosts like to scare 'em. But bats just fly through them. Altogether too much imagination, humans.'

That made sense. If I met a ghost, I'd probably start running and never stop. 'So, what sort of ghosts?' I asked.

'What sort of ghosts? What like kind of a question is that? Ghosts is ghosts is ghosts. Dead people. Go in for haunting a lot, style of thing?'

'I mean, what sort of people were they?'

'What sort of people? People, people! Two legs, two arms, the usual. There's the odd ghost dog or cat about, and a rat or two, but animals, they mostly sleep. It's just the dead humans that do the old moaning and wailing.'

Just then the air around us whirred and Gwydion and Gwyddno flapped silently up to perch beside us.

'Who's your friend?' Gwydion asked.

'Diarmuid Bat at your service,' my suitor introduced himself. 'And there was me thinking this fine young thing was fancy free and here you are, wrecking my chances. Unless you're her brother and her Da, would that be it?' he enquired hopefully.

'No, we're not,' Gwydion said, looking menacing and stretching his wings to their leathery fullness. 'And I'd be quite grateful if you'd buzz off.'

'What style of bats are youse?' Diarmuid complained. 'Thinking bats buzz! Suspicious, you lot are!'

Gwydion twitched his whiskers and looked so menacing that Diarmuid Bat decided to roost elsewhere. He flapped disconsolately out of the attic with a hurt backward glance at me.

'What did you find out?' I asked.

Gwydion settled his wings and dangled. 'Not a lot. Just that the castle is full of absolutely nothing except dust and decaying furniture.'

I bent my wing and inspected my thumbnail casually. 'Wrong! This is the Black Castle of Ballygar, and it's full of ghosts.'

'Pull the other one, Tanz. It's got bells on.'

'No, honestly. Well, I *think* so. The bat said that only humans can see them, because humans are afraid of them. And they really like scaring humans.'

Gwyddno shuffled nervously closer to Gwydion. 'Ghosts? I can't say I'm in favour of ghosts. Of course, I've never seen one, but you wouldn't catch me walking through a graveyard at midnight, I can tell you.'

'You don't have to. Apparently, the whole castle is full of them. They are probably watching us now. The thing is, we won't see them unless we're human. And I've got this really horrible feeling that the only way we are going to find Elffin and T.A. is to be human and look for them. And that means facing the ghosts.'

'Oh.' Gwyddno turned pale, and Gwydion twitched a bit.

'What we have to remember,' I said, more confident than I actually felt, 'is that ghosts can't hurt us. They're only sort of ex-people, right? They don't have bodies, so they can't do anything. Just grit your teeth and keep walking. Tell yourself that somewhere in this castle your son, Gwyddno, and my best friend are waiting for us. Now, come on.'

We dropped off our beam and fluttered down to the dusty floor. I closed my eyes and shifted. For all my bravado, and leading the way sort of stuff, I was a bit reluctant to open my eyes again. When I did, the air was *thick*.

It was also very, very cold, for all that it was summer outside. I could see my breath smoking on the air. Goosebumps popped up on my arms and I could feel the hair at the nape of my neck prickling. If it hadn't been long, it would probably have been standing on end.

All round us were *shapes*. People shapes, clustering and staring. Hundreds and hundreds of them, jostling like a herd of insubstantial cows. I gritted my teeth and started walking.

Through them. Literally. They parted like smoke, a head and arms in one direction, the rest of the body in another, to rejoin once I'd passed. Some of them were just wreaths of person-shaped mist, others were altogether more substantial, with a distinct outline of the person they'd once been. I could distinguish clothes, faces with moustaches and beards, expressions, and women with long hair floating round their faces. Their eyes weren't actually eyes, just dark spaces in their filmy heads, but inside each pair of eye-spaces a light glinted far off. They could see me – probably much clearer than I could see them, and they were much more distinct than I'd have liked!

'Ooooooooh!' one said creakily, as if it hadn't used its voice for a long, long time. 'Aaaaaaaaaagh! Grooooaaaannnn.' Then it coughed, with lungs it didn't have . . .

A rattle of chains, and the sound of metal dragging across a stone floor. A door creaked open and a cold wind rushed in my face. Ghostly figures massed and milled, clammy touches of mist stroked my face, howls and wails and moans echoed eerily in my ears and I was just about to decide to get really, really scared, and maybe even make a run for it when I got cross instead.

'Oh for goodness sake!' I said loudly. '*Will* you cut this out? It isn't big, it isn't clever, and you aren't scaring us one bit, so you might as well stop right now. Just tell us where T.A. and Elffin are, and then we can get out of here and you can get on with haunting someone who cares!'

There was a moment's pindrop silence.

'What did she say?' asked a voice, plaintively. 'Did she say she's not scared, Tomás?'

'She did so, Michéal. I heard her with my very own ears, I did.'

'Ah, you don't have ears!'

'I do so. Are they not one each side of the head I once had?'

'The one that's stuck on the battlements for all time, is that the head you're referring to, Tomás?'

'It is, and it's terrible cruel of you to remind me of my shortcomings, Michéal.'

'But did the girl say she's not afraid, Tomás?'

'Have we not had this conversation before Michéal?'

'Then we have to help her, do we not, Tomás?'

'That's the rules, Michéal. If they are not afraid of us, then we have to help them. So, girl, what do you want?'

I tried to focus on the one called Michéal, who seemed to have a bit of common sense, and at least had some sort of a head to talk to. He was a bit on the bleary side, but after a while I got the hang of focussing on him sort of out of the corners of my eyes, and he was clearer. He'd probably been quite good-looking when he was alive. 'We're looking for two people. Conor of the Land Beneath captured them, and is holding them prisoner. A girl and a boy. We've looked everywhere in the castle, but we can't find them. Do you know where they are?'

'Conor of the Land Beneath, is it?' Michéal said disapprovingly. 'Nasty wee piece of work, that one. We have some of his handiwork here, we do so.'

'Handiwork?' Gwydion said, mystified.

'Didn't he hunt down and kill Big Deirdre's cub? We've got the poor, bewildered wee thing wandering around, since he was struck down just outside the gates of the place. Wandered in and can't go home, never stops crying for his Mammy, he does not. If I can poke one finger in Conor's eye, I'll do it, and if I can poke two, then I shall be happy indeed.'

'So, do you know where T.A. and Elffin are?'

'Would she be a pretty bit of a dark-haired thing, and him and her both of the Welsh persuasion?'

'That's them!' I yelled ungrammatically.

'Don't have a single idea where they might be, no not at all,' Micheál said.

'What? But you just described them. You must have seen them!'

'I have so. Scared the boy stiff as a plank, so I did, but the wee girl, she stood up to me and told me off for making such noise when they were trying to sleep. Sure, weren't they sleeping downstairs in the drawing room where Conor left them?'

I tried to ungrit my teeth and speak in a pleasant voice, but I was getting distinctly ratty. 'So where are they now?'

'Didn't Conor put a spell upon the two of them? They're here – but they aren't here at all, either.'

I put my head in my hands and wished I was elsewhere, preferably tucked up in bed and dreaming this. 'They're here, but they aren't.'

'Isn't that just what I said?'

'Yes, but it doesn't make any sense.' And then, suddenly, it did. Even the key we'd stolen from Conor suddenly made sense – or so I thought, anyway. At least, something had clicked into place in my mind. 'They're here, but they aren't!' I said to Gwydion and Gwyddno, triumphantly. 'I think I know where they are!'

'Well, isn't that intelligent, so,' Michéal said proudly. 'Didn't I know you were a good style of person altogether, with the marvellous brains and all. Now, if there's nothing else I can help you with, we have to go and re-do the sinister on the walls. Needs another coat, so it does, and some of those old bones need a bit of a dust. Never a moment's rest in this benighted place, there is not, always something needing to be done.'

The ghostly company dispersed, and the three of us live people got in a huddle.

'So, Tanz, what's your idea?' Gwydion asked.

'It's the same as when you were kidnapped, Gwyd,' I said excitedly, 'if they are here and aren't here at the same time, then they have to be in a Time Door, right?'

Gwyddno looked bemused. 'I don't understand,' he said. 'I can see how ghosts can be here and not here at the same time, but people?'

'That's because you don't know about Time Doors, Gwyddno,' Gwydion explained. 'We do, because of our magic. They are doors where the fabric of the universe thins, where the space/time continuum twitches and turns like a Mobiüs strip –'

'Pardon?' Gwyddno said.

I folded my arms. 'Now where did you get that from, Gwyd? You must have pinched it from somewhere!'

'Oh, all right. I read it in a book once, when I was in your Time. Haven't got a clue what it means. Sounds impressive though, doesn't it? You see, Gwyddno, there are doors that let you go forward or back in time. They're all over Ynys Haf, and all over Tanith's Time, too. When you find one, you can get through very quickly going in, but it takes ages the other way about. You can quite literally get stuck in them if you don't obey the rules.'

'But T.A. knows perfectly well that you mustn't turn round in a Time Door, because you get trapped there until someone lets you out,' I said. 'She wouldn't do that, and if they were going into a Time Door, she'd certainly have warned Elffin about it.'

'Unless they didn't know they were in one until it was too late,' Gwydion said thoughtfully. 'So, where is it?'

'I suppose we start looking, right?'

8

This time we weren't looking for people, but for a Time Door, and so we went through the Black Castle as ourselves, which was a bit more tiring than flitting round it as bats. Until, that is, I got the idea of *floating* up the spiral staircases instead of tramping up and down them. That speeded the search considerably, but was so fast that after floating up and down a couple of spiral staircases I started to feel a bit air-sick.

We searched that place again from cellars to attic, looking for the thin bit of air that betrays a Time Door. Sometimes, if the light is just right, you can catch a sort of after-image of a door. If you can't imagine that, try looking briefly at a light bulb, and then close your eyes. You can still see the after-image of the light, can't you? Well, that's what spotting Time Doors is like.

But neither Gwydion nor I could see anything remotely like a Time Door.

'Are you certain there's one here, Tanz?' he asked after our second pass through.

'Michéal said that they were here – and not here, both at once. So somewhere there's a Time Door. There has to be. Come on, let's look again.'

'No,' Gwyddno said. 'I can't climb any more spiral staircases. Not ever. When I get home I'm going to have every single one in Cantre'r Gwaelod ripped out and put in ladders instead.'

'You wait here,' I said, feeling a bit sorry for him. He hadn't got the hang of floating and had walked up them all. 'Gwydion and I will have another hunt. There has to be one somewhere.'

So off we went again. We looked in every single room, moved chairs and tables and got covered in thick, choking dust. We prodded inside cupboards, pulled back wall-hangings, poked under beds. At last, out on the black battlements, I slumped against a wall in despair. 'If it's here I'm blowed if I can see it. There's nowhere else to look, Gwyd.' We were at the back of the Castle, and I draped myself over the wall to see the view. Surprisingly, there was a moat at the back, although not at the front, so on the whole it was fairly useless as a defence. The water reflected the black castle walls and looked cold, oily and sinister. Something reddish-brown projecting from the wall at the base of the castle, at moat level, caught my eye. I leaned over, dislodging a grinning skull, which splashed into the moat, shattering the glassy surface.

'Gwyd, there's a water-gate down there!'

'A what?'

'A water-gate. You know, a place where people can reach the moat from inside the castle.'

He stared at me.

'Come on,' I said, and headed for the spiral stairs again. It took some finding, that watergate. In the end we had to go back down into the cellars, out of one of the doors in the wall, up a short flight of (mercifully straight) steps, across the drawbridge and into the open air. Sure enough, there was the water-gate, the tell-tale rusted hinge I'd spotted sticking out. The trouble was, it was on the other side of the moat. I thought about swimming across for at least two seconds, and then thought about what might be lurking below the oily surface of the water, and changed my mind. I magicked a boat, Gwydion and I climbed in, and he rowed us across to the water-gate. Being made of iron, of course, neither of us could touch it, and even bobbing about on the moat that close to it made me feel ill. So we rowed back again to fetch Gwyddno, who had no magic at all, and rowed him across. He had the gate open in a trice, and shoved it straight back across the wall so that we could pass through without touching it.

We were in a small turret room with a door in the far wall. The door was padlocked and banded with iron, but that didn't matter, because just to the right of it, on the curved wall, was the tell-tale shimmer of air.

'Gotcha!' I said smugly. 'Gwyddno, you stay here. I don't want to risk you going into the Time Door. We'll go in, find T.A. and Elffin and be right back. I hope we won't be long, but you can never tell with these things.'

Gwyddno gulped. 'Bring back my son, Lady,' he said.

I grinned. 'You bet! See you!'

Gwydion and I stepped into the Doorway. We'd taken only a few steps when the wind hit us. I always forget between the times that I use the Doors how powerful that wind is. Imagine the strongest gust you've ever experienced, and multiply it by ten. To walk against it, you have to bend double, and it puffs out your cheeks, makes your eyes water and steals your breath. It was slightly easier for me, because I cheated and walked behind Gwydion. I pushed him, mind, so that helped a bit. We hadn't gone far when Gwydion let out a whoop of joy.

'They're here!' he yelled. 'T.A! Elffin! Wake up!'

We drew level with the slumped bodies and knelt beside them, careful to keep our backs to the entrance. We would have to go all the way out to the other Time and then step back inside. Still, the journey would be instant the other way, it always is. I shook T.A.'s shoulder, but she didn't stir, and Gwydion was having no luck with Elffin, either.

'I think they've been enchanted or something, Tanz,' he said worriedly. 'We'll have to get them outside and try to wake them up.'

'Well, I can't carry T.A. on my own. She's too heavy. We'll have to carry them out one at a time.'

So we picked up T.A., her arms stretched over our shoulders, and heaved her along the Time tunnel to the outside world. We stepped into daylight and snow, and it looked as if we'd somehow arrived in Switzerland or somewhere! 'Good grief, I wonder where we are?' I muttered.

Gwydion was grinning. 'I know exactly where we are,' he said. 'Down there in the valley is a little place called Blaengwynfi. Remind me to tell you about some friends I made here, Tanz. A boy called Maldwyn and a girl called Betsan. Mind, I expect they're grown up by now.' He shook his head, smiling soppily. 'Wow, that was an adventure! Wonder if they remember me?'

'Adventure?' I snapped. 'This is no time for happy memories, Gwyd. We have to go back and get Elffin, and quick before T.A. freezes to death.' We dumped her unceremoniously in the snow and dived back into the Time Door. Instantly, because of course we had to go all the way through or get stuck ourselves, we popped out in the tower room where an anxious Gwyddno Garanhir awaited us.

'Where's my boy?' he asked, grabbing Gwydion by the jacket. 'Where's Elffin?'

'We've found him, don't worry, but we've got to go back in. We'll be back as soon as we can.'

We dived back into the Time Door, and once again headed into the mighty wind. When we came to Elffin, we heaved him up onto our shoulders to drag him out of the tunnel (it would have been easier if Gwydion could have taken his head and me his feet or something, but that would have meant one of us walking backwards, right?). As we picked him up, I noticed that he was clutching a small, silver-bound wooden box. It fell from his hand, and I picked it up, shoved it inside my jerkin and helped Gwydion drag the unconscious young man outside. We dumped him on the grass beside T.A. I put the box down and patted her face.

'T.A., wake up! Come on, you can't stay here.'

'If there's a spell on her, Tanz, would you know?'

'I ought to. Unless it's an Irish one, of course. We only managed to wake you up because of O'Liam when you were stuck in a Time Door.'

'Do you think it's the same one? Can you remember it?'

'I'm not sure if it's the same, but fortunately I filed it away in my witch-memory for future reference. I'll give it a whirl – *if* I can get the pronunciation right! Erse isn't that easy, you know!'

I put my hand on T.A.'s forehead, closed my eyes

and concentrated on remembering the sound of the words that O'Liam had uttered. They came flooding back, and tentatively, and then with more confidence as my memory kicked in, I said them:

> *'Duine atá I do chodladh, aithnim duit muscailt*
> *arraingt anáil mhór amháin*
> *Duine atá id o Chodladh, aithnim duit muscailt.'*

> Sleeper, I ask you to wake
> One full breath do take
> Sleeper, I bid you wake.'

Worked like a charm! T.A. was awake instantly, and started complaining about the cold as her eyes opened, which was understandable, since she was only wearing a thin summer robe and was rapidly turning blue. I magicked her a warm coat and scarf, topped the lot off with a bobble hat in a fetching shade of puce, and turned my attention to Elffin.

As soon as he was back with us, we re-entered the Time Door, the little wooden chest still tucked safely inside my top.

We stepped out into the gloomy turret room, and Gwyddno Garanhir fell upon his son with a bellow of joy. When he'd finished hugging him, he gave him such a clout on the back of the head that Elffin's eyes crossed.

'Don't you ever, *ever* go off on a wild goose chase like that again,' his father thundered. 'I'll personally dismember you if you do! Just because a pretty face asks you, is no reason to put your whole life in danger, you stupid boy!'

'Yes, Dada,' Elffin said meekly. 'No, Dada. I won't do it again, Dada.'

T.A. looked indignant. Couldn't see why – he'd said she had a pretty face, hadn't he?

'Elffin insisted on coming,' she said mutinously. 'I told him I'd be perfectly all right on my own, but he wouldn't let me.'

'Hmm.' Gwyddno's furious expression softened. 'Well, he wouldn't be my boy if he wasn't brave and gallant, and with an eye for a pretty *merch*, I suppose.' Nevertheless, he gave Elffin another wallop. 'But don't do it again without telling me first, all right?'

Elffin grinned. 'No, Dad.' Then he spotted the wooden box, now tucked under my arm. 'Oh, you brought that. Good. Conor left it behind when he took us into the Time Door. He put it on the floor before he enchanted us. The last thing I remember doing is scooping it into my arms. What's in it?'

I shook the box. It rattled, very faintly. I tried to open it, but it was locked, and although the chest was made of wood, it was very firmly bound with silver bands so that it would be hard to get into even with a chisel. 'Don't know,' I said, giving it another experimental rattle. 'it's locked, and there isn't a –'

Light dawned on both Gwydion and me simultaneously.

'– key!' I finished, grinning.

Gwydion grinned back. 'What's the betting that's very, very precious to Conor of the Land Beneath?' he said happily. 'And now we've got it, and we've almost certainly got the key to it, too!'

'You have? How?' T.A. asked, stripping off the

puce bobble hat and winter coat and dumping them on the floor.

'O'Liam's Mammy told us we'd need it, so we stole it from Conor. We hid it, and we know exactly where it is, and all we've got to do is go back and find it, open the box, and see what Conor's secrets are!'

We shifted into birds – the others into starlings and I a buzzard, so I could carry the precious box in my talons. Then we were through the watergate and flying off. Gwydion led the way back to the tree where he'd hidden the three silvery keys safely in a squirrel's drey. We shifted back on the ground while Gwydion flew up to the drey and hopped inside. I stood beneath the tree, waiting to catch the keys as he threw them down.

Except he didn't. He flew down beside me and shifted back. His eyebrows were drawn together in a thunderous line.

'They're gone!' he said angrily.

9

'They can't be!' I protested.

'You want to go and look?'

'No. I believe you. But where can they be?'

Gwydion shrugged. 'How should I know? All I know is that we put them in that drey, and they aren't there now.'

'Are you sure it's the same tree? The same drey?'

'Absolutely. I remember this broken branch, here, and there's a magpie's nest halfway up, and –'

'Magpie?' T.A. was looking thoughtful.

'Magpie. So it's definitely the same tree, Tanz.'

'Magpie,' T.A. repeated.

'Yes, T.A., magpie. Magpie. Black and white bird. Think Astarte Perkins,' Gwydion said crossly.

'Think yourself, chum,' she said. 'Think magpies. Think character. Don't think Astarte Perkins. Think magpie-the-bird.'

'What about them?'

'Magpies just love bright, shiny things, right?'

'Well, yes, but –'

'So what better candidate to nick your keys than a magpie. Check the nest. Go on, humour me.'

Gwydion looked doubtful, but shifted again and flew up to the magpie's nest. Seconds later, one after the other, three small silver shapes dropped to the piney forest floor with satisfying plops. T.A. looked smug.

I picked up the keys, and tried them one after the other in the lock. The first one was too big, the second

was the right size but wouldn't turn, and the third –
not surprisingly – both fitted and turned. The lock
opened with a faint click, and the others gathered
round as I raised the silver-banded lid.

Inside were two smaller boxes. One rattled, the
other didn't. I opened the first. And then, totally
mystified, the other. We all stared at each other. Then
back at the contents of the little boxes, and then back
at each other again.

'What on earth –?' T.A. said.

Inside the first box was a large collection of nail
clippings.

The second was crammed full to bursting with short
bits of golden hair!

'Why in the world would Conor of the Land
Beneath go to so much trouble to hide his off-cuts?'
T.A. asked, bewilderedly, rattling the box with the
fingernails in.

'Yuk!' I said, and was about to chuck the stuff
away, when me-the-witch suddenly kicked in. 'Wait a
minute!' I said, and could feel a grin spreading across
my face. 'I think I've got it!'

'What?' the others said together.

'What gives someone power over someone else?
How did I make the Maebh-golem, Gwyd?'

His face cleared as he saw where my mind was
heading. 'Bits of personal stuff, like fingernail
clippings and hair. If they're moulded into wax dolls
the person they belong to is in your power.'

'And what would Conor do to recover this, do you
think?'

'Just about anything, I'd imagine.' Gwydion

grinned at me. 'I think we've got the little rat where we want him. Even if the fake Maebh disintegrates into straw and mud tomorrow, there isn't a thing he can do to us.'

'Except of course he's still got O'Liam's Mammy as a hostage, and O'Liam's promised to go back for a month and a day every year to ironfind for him.'

'There is that. But at least this gives us some bargaining power.'

'So,' T.A. said, 'what do we do now?'

'The first thing we do is get home,' I said. 'Then Gwydion and I can mop up Spiderwitch and this whole horrible affair will be over. Always assuming that Merlin has managed to sort out the drought in Ynys Haf.'

Now, you might imagine that this sensible thing us just what we did, right? Straight away, done, finito, all that stuff. But then, you'll know that life – especially *my* life – is never quite that easy, is it?

We were all exhausted, so we decided to fly back in the morning. It was going to be a long journey – Ballygar was almost two-thirds of the way across Ireland, and besides, I thought we deserved a bit of a feast and a treat. So we made camp for the night in some very snazzy sleeping bags inside an even snazzier tent (which impressed Gwyddno and Elffin mightily) and I magicked up a meal that would even have beaten O'Liam of the Green Boots (and the Little Round Belly, these days!). And when we'd eaten all the goodies and drunk all the liquid, and some of it was alcohol, yes, because Gwyddno enjoys a good glass of wine, and it would have been rude to let him drink it *all* by himself, we snuggled down in our snazzy sleeping bags and went . . . to . . . sleep.

And slept late. And woke, each with our own private headache. We ate a light breakfast and then I disappeared the sleeping bags and looked around the tent for the little silver-bound chest.

'Does anyone remember moving Conor's box last night?' I asked, poking around the tent corners.

'No. I thought you put it over there,' T.A. said, pointing.

'Well, it isn't there now.' I magicked the sleeping bags back, just in case it had got caught up in one of them, but it hadn't. 'Gwydion, Gwyddno, Elffin, have you moved it?'

They shook their heads and helped look. But it doesn't take long to search a tent, even a snazzy one with separate sleeping compartments and a portapotti in a little striped hut outside. We very quickly realised that Conor's box with its precious contents was missing. My spirits thumped down into the soles of my feet. Someone had stolen our Secret Weapon.

'Who would steal that?' Gwyddno asked.

I shrugged. 'Not a clue. The only enemies we've got here are Conor and Big Deirdre. Deirdre's probably miles away, guarding her port, and if Conor took it back he wouldn't have missed the opportunity to do something nasty to us while he was here. He wouldn't just have taken it. By now we'd be locked up somewhere ironclad. Or dead. Anybody else got any ideas?'

Nobody had, and so we decided to head back to

Ynys Haf anyway, to try and sort things out there. At least most of my problems would have been solved. Only the Maebh problem was still out there. Once the fake Maebh disintegrated, Conor was not going to be a happy leprechaun. That was still down to me. I still owed him Maebh, and he would be determined to have her one way or another. However, I was equally determined that he shouldn't. It's what they call a Mexican stand-off. Or maybe a Welsh one, I don't know.

Disconsolately I disappeared the tent, and was squinting miserably into the morning sun, when something caught my eye. As the tent disappeared into thin air, something that had been inside it floated softly down to the ground, glinting in the brightness. I bent over, and searched the flattened grass. At first I couldn't see it, and then I could.

A spiderweb. A large, thick spiderweb. Not as thick as the one that had been in Merch Corryn Du's cave, but thicker than normal. It made me thoughtful. Maybe, just maybe . . .

'Gwydion,' I called, 'come here a minute, please.'

I showed him the fragmented web clinging to the grass. 'You don't suppose Spiderwitch is about, do you?'

He peered at the web, poked it with his finger. 'It's possible. After all, she wasn't in Bugsy's nest, and she wasn't in her cave. She has to be somewhere, and once she was free of the dragon, it would be no problem for her to get across to Erin.' He looked up, and our eyes met. 'And if Spiderwitch and Conor of the Land Beneath get together . . .' he said, thoughtfully,

Oh, dear.

'Then,' he mused, 'she will know straight away that his Maebh is a fake. And worse, she'll tell him, and he'll be furious and on the warpath, and the first thing he'll do is probably head for Ynys Haf with a great big army of leprechauns to take revenge. That's terrible, Tanz! What are we going to do?'

'It may not be as terrible as all that, Gwyd. Think about it – if Spiderwitch has Conor's fingernails and stuff, and he thinks she's on his side . . .'

Gwydion caught my train of thought. 'She'll have him in her power, won't she? And he won't even know that whatever happens to Ynys Haf, win or lose, she's got control.'

'Right,' I said grimly, 'she'll get him to risk everything, his kingdom, all his people, to take over the Island of Summer, and then she'll finish him off. And Spiderwitch will be in control of our land, and we'll have to fight her for it. Gwydion, we can't let that happen.'

Just when we'd thought we were winning, the whole affair had turned round and bitten us. We had to do some fast thinking, and try to get back on top. The problem was where to begin.

'Are we going to tell the others, Gwydion?' I asked softly, glancing at where T.A., Elffin and Gwyddno were sitting quietly holding their heads and waiting for us to finish talking and magic them and their hangovers back to Ynys Haf.

'We must. They have a right to know. Gwyddno will have to fight to protect Cantre'r Gwaelod –'

'Hang about, Gwydion,' I said, a thought striking

me, 'we know exactly what happens to Cantre'r Gwaelod, and Gwyddno is still Lord when it does, so –'

'Yes, but we don't know when, do we?' Gwydion said.

I couldn't bear to think of it. One day Cantre'r Gwaelod would disappear beneath the waves – perhaps soon. Gwyddno would die. And Elffin. Only Taliesin would survive.

'So if we keep Gwyddno Garanhir and Elffin here, then Cantre'r Gwaelod – and they – are safe. Is that it?'

Gwydion shrugged, miserably. 'I don't know, Tanz. All I know is we can't change anything. Merlin is definite about that. Says we can't, we mustn't even try. But isn't this an emergency that over-rides all that?'

I stared at him, wishing there were someone very old and very wise we could ask. I know, you're probably thinking 'Ask Merlin', right? But would Merlin help us? He was always concerned only with Ynys Haf itself. Not us, not the people, just the country. It looked very much as if we were entirely on our own.

10

'What are we going to do? Are you certain that everybody dies?'

'Gwyddno Garanhir and everybody that is in Cantre'r Gwaelod at –' he caught his breath and stared at me. '– at the time!' he finished, and I felt that there might be a teeny, squinchy bit of hope.

'So if we can evacuate Cantre'r Gwaelod before the disaster, there won't be anyone there and no one will drown, right?'

'I don't know. But how are we supposed to persuade everyone in the Sixteen Cities to leave – without a good reason?'

'We could try.'

'It wouldn't work. Remember, in the legend it says that Gwyddno has this great big party and invites everyone in the Sixteen Cities except Seithennyn, the sluice-gate keeper. He gets ratty about being left out, drinks too much and forgets to close the gates so that the high tide comes in. Oh, Tanz, there must be some way round it. We'll think about it later. In the meantime, we have to keep Gwyddno with us, for a start – that way we know he and Cantre'r Gwaelod are safe, don't we? At least for a while.'

I sighed. It was decision time. 'Gwydion, I think we'd better stop rushing about like headless chickens, and – well, I suppose there's nothing else for it but to head for the Land Beneath and try to find out if Spiderwitch has got there already.'

'And if she's told Conor about the fake Maebh,' Gwydion muttered.

'So what do we do? Go in and brazen it out, or sneak in and see what's happening?' I asked.

'Oh, I think sneaky does it, don't you?' Gwydion managed a grin, but I could tell he wasn't feeling particularly happy.

'Who's going to break it to the others?' I said. 'Gwyddno's going to want to go home, but we can't let him or Elffin go near the place until we're with them, can we? And if they go back, they'll want to take T.A. with them, and that will put her in danger. So they've all got to stay with us. Which leaves them open to attack by Conor of the Land Beneath and quite probably Spiderwitch as well. Oh, Gwydion, it's such a mess!'

'You can say that again,' the Dragonking said disconsolately. 'You can just say that again!'

I didn't, of course. I wasn't in the mood for old jokes. Gwydion reached out and took my hand – whether it was for comfort for him or for me I wasn't quite sure, but it did the trick anyway. I gave it a squeeze and he squeezed back, his big palm warm and dry.

Gwyddno looked up as we approached the group on the grass. 'Are we going home now?' he asked plaintively. 'I think I could do with one of the headache powders my wife makes. She puts betony in it, and wine and honey, and peppercorns, I think.'

'Bit of a hair of the dog, eh?' T.A. said with a grin.

Gwyddno frowned. 'No, I don't think she puts dog hair in it. I don't think I could stomach dog hair.'

Then T.A. noticed our expressions. 'What?' she said suspiciously.

'Well,' I began, 'I'm afraid that we can't go back to Ynys Haf right now. It's possible Spiderwitch is here in the Land Beneath. And with her on Conor's side – even if she isn't, if you see what I mean, but he thinks she is – well, we daren't waste time taking you back until we know what they're up to. Sorry and all that, but –'

Gwyddno looked unhappy, but T.A. and Elffin cheered up immediately. 'More adventure? Goodie!' T.A. crowed, and she and Elffin high-fived each other. When had she taught him *that*?

'Forget adventure, you two. Don't imagine for one minute that we're going to risk taking you into the Land Beneath again,' Gwydion said. 'Oh no. You two are staying outside where it's safe.'

'Outside, eh,' T.A. said, a gleam in her eye. 'Outside where there's Pwca Horses and Great Worms and Terrible Beasts and stuff. Not to mention Big Deirdre and the Banshee.'

'If you three stay put, there's no earthly reason why you should run into any one of them,' Gwydion said firmly. 'And you *will* stay put even if I have to turn you into trees to do it!'

'Spoilsport!' T.A. muttered.

'All the same,' Gwydion insisted. 'You are going to promise to behave yourself, T.A., and you, Elffin, or it's trees, right? Promise?'

Elffin and T.A. glanced at each other. 'Promise,' they said sweetly.

It didn't do any good. I was already round behind them.

'Now uncross your fingers and promise,' I ordered.
They did.

'Right. You've promised.' I looked stern and Lady-like. 'So all three of you stay where we put you and don't move unless it's a real emergency. Got that?'

'Yes,' my friend said sullenly.

I know, I know. I left her a loophole, didn't I?

Anyway, we shifted them all and we flew as close as we could to the entrance to the Land Beneath without being spotted by any of Conor's guards, landed and parked the three mortals in a small cave halfway up a hillside. I reminded them yet again that they'd promised to stay put.

'Yes, Tanz,' T.A. said demurely.

I looked suspiciously at her.

'We heard what you said,' she said, 'don't worry.'

All the same, I did. I know T.A. too well.

Gwydion and I crept towards the Land Beneath and became, once more, ants. This was the safest shape to take: small, unobtrusive and fast. If Superwitch had got to Conor of the Land Beneath, then we could sneak back out again and try to decide what to do.

We scuttled under the door and went looking. We found Conor in his Trophy Room, surrounded by those horrible heads – including Big Deirdre's poor cub, who may have been a giant and not exactly fluffy-bunny cute, but he was still her baby, and didn't deserve to be hunted and killed by a nasty little leprechaun.

The nasty leprechaun in question was pacing the room, hands behind his back, looking worried. A wizened little chap with a long, wispy grey beard and a black robe stood before him, clutching a book to his chest like a shield.

Conor scowled at him. 'Call yourself a physician?' he hissed, 'when you can't even wake somebody up?'

'Oh, my lord,' stammered the old leprechaun, 'I swear we have tried every mortal thing, we have so, but the princess does not open her eyes. The only thing we have not tried is the kiss of a handsome prince, but you tried that yourself, have you not, my Lord, and none more handsome than you, no, not at all, my Lord, and even that did nothing to remedy the situation, it did not, and so there is nothing more that I can suggest, no nothing whatsoever. We are completely baffled.'

'And completely useless!' Conor shrieked, and the old man flinched. 'Get from my sight now, old man, before I decide to punish you as you deserve!'

'Ooh, temper, temper!' I whispered to Gwydion, and he nudged me with a feeler.

'It sounds as if Maebh is still asleep,' he whispered back.

'And that Spiderwitch isn't here!' I crowed.

And then –

She was.

11

She hadn't improved much, that was for sure. The black hair was still coiled like a boa constrictor on top of her head, and the red-glass spectacles still masked her eyes. She wore a long black dress with wispy bits dangling off it like spiders' legs, and her movements were quick and scuttling.

Conor looked up, saw her, and sprang to his feet. 'How did you get in here?' he hissed. 'Guards!'

Merch Corryn Du smiled an unpleasant smile. 'That doesn't matter, Conor of the Land Beneath. I am in. Don't you know by now how powerful I am?'

'Guards!' Conor screamed, rushing towards the door. It didn't help, not at all. Half a dozen assorted men at arms crashed into the chamber and skidded to a terrified halt.

'Take her away! Lock her in the dungeons! Chain her with iron chains!' Conor screamed.

The men at arms shifted from foot to foot and looked at each other. None of them looked at Conor. 'Ah,' one of them said at last. 'Would this be the Spider Queen herself, now?'

'It would indeed,' Spiderwitch agreed, folding her long, thin arms across her black chest. 'Shall I prove it?'

'Ah,' the man said again, nervously. 'Sure, and that won't be necessary at all, your Spidership. If that'll be all, we'll be away now. Nice meeting you, and all that, it is so!'

'Take her away and lock her up, I said,' Conor hissed, 'or it will go badly with you!'

One of the unhappy guards took a step towards Spiderwitch, perhaps a little more afraid of Conor than he was of her. BIG mistake.

Spiderwitch pointed a long, crimson-nailed finger at him, and he shrivelled. By the time she'd finished, he was just a dried-up leprechaun husk. Rather like the dead flies you see hanging about in old spiderwebs . . .

It did the trick, though. The others backed enthusiastically away, heading smartly for the door and escape.

'Gooood boys!' Spiderwitch purred, and prodded what was left of their comrade with her shoe. 'Take the rubbish with you, please.'

Two of them plucked up courage to go near enough to Spiderwitch to pick up the desiccated remnants of their comrade, and carried him out. The door closed behind them, and there was the sound of running feet. Spiderwitch turned her attention to Conor. She towered over him, staring menacingly through her crimson eye-pieces.

'Now, little man,' she began, 'let us talk.'

'I have nothing to say to you,' Conor squeaked. 'This is my kingdom. You have no rights here, no, none at all!'

Spiderwitch sneered. 'No rights, you say? Would you like to put that to the test, my undersized friend?'

Conor looked sullen. He knew his magic wasn't anywhere near as strong as hers, but he made up for it with a great talent for being sneaky and untrustworthy. If he was wise, he'd bide his time. I *almost* felt sorry for him.

'Good,' Spiderwitch purred. 'Now, I believe that you have my grand-daughter here.'

Conor nodded. 'What if I have? Anyway, she's sick. She won't wake up. Some style of spell has been put upon her.'

'Sick?' Spiderwitch scowled. 'Impossible. She doesn't get sick. I don't allow it.'

I had a feeling I knew what was coming next. I was right.

'Where is she?' Spiderwitch demanded.

With Conor leading the way, and Gwydion and me scuttling along behind Spiderwitch, trying to be unobtrusive, we made our way to Conor's guest chamber, where the fake Maebh lay smiling vacantly, her eyes shut.

Spiderwitch crossed to the bed. 'Get up at once, you stupid girl!' she ordered. 'You know perfectly well you are not allowed to lie in bed in the middle of the day!'

Maebh, not surprisingly, didn't even twitch.

Spiderwitch's voice and temper rose a notch. 'I told you to get up!' she screamed. 'This is your Great-great-great-great-Granny *commanding* you!'

The fake Maebh slumbered on. Spiderwitch reached out a finger and prodded the sleeping figure. Hard.

'You see?' Conor said. 'Not with us at all. Off with the fairies, she is so.'

'Off with the fairies? You stupid little leprechaun! This isn't Maebh! I knew it the instant I touched her. This is a fake! A fake made of straw and mud and fingernail clippings! Someone has made a fool of you! How could you imagine that this – this – thing is related to me? By the great god Tarantula, it's hard enough to imagine when it's the real thing!'

'Oh-oh!' Gwydion and I muttered together.

'Now who,' Spiderwitch mused, tapping her red fingernail on her pointed teeth. 'could have done this, do you imagine?'

Conor's golden face turned dark. 'I know exactly who. Was it not the Lady of Ynys Haf herself? She promised me I should have Maebh. She promised me! She lied! Ooh, when I lay my hands on her, she will suffer, so she will. How dare she cheat me? Me! Conor, Lord of the Land Beneath! Isn't it me that's supposed to cheat, and no one else!'

My anty feet started to make movements towards the nearest exit, but Gwydion put out his feelers and stopped me. 'They don't know we're here,' he whispered. 'We need to find out what they're going to do.'

'Do? They're going to marmalise me, that's what they're going to do!' I said, panicking.

'Calm down, Tanz. She doesn't know we're here. They both think we're miles away, in Ynys Haf, right? And anyway, you're the Lady. You're just as powerful as she is, aren't you?'

'Oh, yes. Right.' Although I didn't feel at all powerful, I calmed down a bit. We tucked ourselves into a shadowy corner and pinned our antennae back.

Spiderwitch paced the chamber, ignoring the fake Maebh. 'So, Conor. We both want revenge on the Lady. Despite the fact that you are nothing but an insignificant pixie, we have a mutual problem. Perhaps we can work together to achieve a solution.'

An insignificant pixie? Ooh, Conor did NOT like that! He had more sense than to say anything, however. But I saw his face close in on itself like a fist, and knew that, whatever plan the two of them came up with, Conor would get his own back for that crack, somehow.

'Perhaps we can, Spiderwitch,' he said softly. 'Perhaps we can.'

Gwydion and I looked at each other, our worst fears realised. Two enemies for the price of one. And no matter how much they hated each other, they'd put it aside until they had attacked Ynys Haf.

Which is what they planned to do. Conor would raise the biggest army that he possibly could. Leprechauns from all over Erin would rise to his call, for he was Lord of them all. Then, with Spiderwitch's magic, they would attack Ynys Haf, and when they had conquered it, they would rule both lands together.

Well, that was what they *agreed*. Since neither trusted the other farther than they could be thrown on a good chucking-day with a strong following wind, however, one of them would end up an ex-person. Possibly a slug or something worse (is there anything worse?). There would be either a Leprechaun King or a Spider Queen ruling both Ynys Haf and the Land Beneath if their plans went well. Somehow I couldn't see them as the perfect partners . . .

We had to stop them. But how?

Gwydion and I made ourselves scarce and scuttled out of the Land Beneath as fast as our legs would carry us. Once in the clearing outside, we shifted into crows and flapped as fast as we could to the place where we'd left T.A., Elffin and Gwyddno Garanhir.

They had company. Somebody small and golden-eyed, wearing magnificent green trainers with flashing lights in the heels.

'O'Liam!' I said, shifting shape, 'what are you doing here?'

He brushed a crow's feather off his jerkin. 'There, and what style of a welcome was that when it's at home? Am I not here where I'm supposed to be, at the side of the Dragonking when he needs me? We have a saying for it, do we not? *There is no need like the lack of a friend*! And am I not a friend, Dragonking?'

'You are indeed,' Gwydion said, and slapped the little man on the shoulder, nearly knocking him out of his trainers. 'We can use all the help we can get, O'Liam.' He looked round the little cave. 'Where's T.A.?'

Elffin shifted uncomfortably. 'Well. Ah. She had this idea, you see.'

I groaned. 'Oh, no! What muddle-headed dumb thing has she done now?'

'It was the sight of Big Deirdre's cub's head in Conor's trophy room that did it,' Elffin said apologetically. 'It made her so mad I couldn't talk her out of it. She said you'd understand what she was doing. Said it was your idea anyway.'

'*My* idea? Well, yes, I may have mentioned it in passing once up on a time,' I said feebly, 'but Big Deirdre will kill her first and ask her what she wants after.'

We needed help, yes, but maybe on reflection Big Deirdre was an ally too far after all. However since T.A. had galloped off madly in all directions, it looked like we'd have to go and rescue her – again. As if we didn't have enough on our plates!

Gwyddno Garanhir looked disgusted. 'I told the little madam she was ill-advised to go down that road,' he said. 'But would she listen? Wouldn't let us go with her, either. Set off at a run, she did, looking for the giant. That's the last you'll see of her, my boy,' he said sternly to Elffin, 'you mark my words. She'll be a giant's breakfast before she knows what's hit her.'

O'Liam groaned. 'And have I just come this whole long way on a wee tippety sickety boat just to find out it's Big Deirdre we're up against first? Ah, why do I bother? We have a saying, so we do, and isn't it the truth? *Go mbeirimid beo ar an am seo arís*, May we be alive this time next year, we say. But if there's the like of a Big Deirdre after us we shall not be!'

'She isn't after you, O'Liam,' I said comfortingly. 'You can stay here with Elffin and Gwyddno while we go and try to find T.A.'

'I will not!' the little man said indignantly. 'What style of a First Leprechaun might I be accused of being if I let the Dragonking go all on his lonesome into the terrible teeth of peril? No, I shall come with you, even though it means my end entirely.'

'And don't think you're leaving me behind, either,' Elffin said. 'Dada, you can stay here if you want, or hop on a boat back to Ynys Haf to warn everybody of what Spiderwitch and Conor are up to – whatever you want to do.'

Gwyddno Garanhir opened and shut his mouth. He was about to object, I think, but his common sense made him see that Elffin's suggestion was probably practical.

'You can get a boat from Deirdre's port,' Gwydion

suggested. 'So we'll shift you and fly you to the coast. You can warn everyone to be on their guard. Make sure the coastal defences are in place, and lookouts are watching for boats.'

'Boats?' O'Liam said. 'Who said anything about boats? They won't come in boats. Spiderwitch and Conor of the Land Beneath in boats? Not a chance. Do you go in a boat if you can change into something that flies or swims? You do not, and neither will they. Your lookouts must watch for magic, not boats. Where is your brain, Lady? And yours, Dragonking? It is magic that you must beware, not fighting men with swords.'

12

But first there was T.A. to rescue. O'Liam and
Gwydion, Elffin, Gwyddno and I all shifted into gulls
and headed for the coast. We flew in a white, gliding
mass, our strong wings rowing the air, the land
unreeling beneath us. First we delivered Gwyddno to a
boatman prepared to take him across the Middlesome
Sea, and then, with the long day drawing redly to a
close, we sailed on upcurrents of warm air to land
close to Big Deirdre's cottage. The goat on the roof
had been joined by a cow, and they watched curiously
as we shimmered and shifted into ourselves, safely out
of sight of the windows.

'I think I should take a look first, before we go
barging in,' I said. 'Gwydion, you stay here.' I
concentrated very hard indeed on damping down my
witchy aura, then shifted into a house-mouse and
scuttled in through the open cottage door. Rich smells
of baking bread tortured my nose, and I realised it was
a long, long time since we'd eaten anything. I hoped
Big Deirdre wouldn't hear my stomach rumbling.

I spotted T.A. at once. She was tied hand and foot
and dumped in a corner. She'd also been gagged, so it
looked like she wasn't having much luck enlisting the
sympathy vote from Big Deirdre!

The large lady in question was of course her normal
size. She had to be, she wouldn't have fitted into the
cottage otherwise. She was sitting at the table with a
mug of steaming tea in front of her, and a familiar
figure sat opposite. Cornelia the Bog Fairy was

stuffing a piece of buttered bread into her mouth and simultaneously sobbing into a large, purple and green spotted hanky, edged with lace.

'And didn't that O'Liam of the Green Boots toy with my womanly emotions, so? Ready I was to give up everything for him, so I was, and he, he, he –' she let loose a miserable wail.

Big Deirdre patted her friend's hand. 'Ah, never mind, never you mind, Cornelia dear. I could never work out what you saw in the wee green creature anyway. Like kissing a wee, skinny frog it would be. But didn't someone wise say there was more good frogs in a pond than ever came out of it?'

'I don't want a frog,' Cornelia wailed, stuffing another piece of bread into her large mouth. 'I want O'Liam of the Green Boots!'

'Well, now patience is a poultice that heals all wounds,' Big Deirdre said. 'And since we have the wee mannie's mortal friend all nice and trussed up in the corner, so, the O'Liam – and the Dragonking and the Lady too as well – will soon be turning up here looking for her, sure as eggs!'

'Eggs, frogs, poultices,' wailed Cornelia. 'All I want is my little man!'

I took advantage of Big Deirdre cutting Cornelia another slice of bread and butter to whisker myself across to T.A. She eyed me, and over the rag that gagged her she didn't look happy. Not fond of mice, our T.A. I grinned a wicked, mousy grin and climbed up her arm. She twitched, and her eyes went wide, but when I reached her shoulder and whispered in her ear, she relaxed and gave me a 'just you wait!' sort of glare. I scuttled down and started gnawing on the ropes that tied her feet. However, they were tough ropes, and it would take too long to chew through them. She'd have to stay tied up a bit longer.

I scuttled back outside and rejoined the others. 'She's in there, tied up,' I told them, 'and so's Big Deirdre and the Bog Fairy. Not tied up, I mean. Just there.'

O'Liam turned on his fancy green trainers with the flashing lights and set off at a run in the away direction. Gwydion grabbed him by the jerkin and hauled him back.

'Leaving my side, First Leprechaun?' he said sternly.

'Oh, Dragonking,' Liam moaned, 'don't make me stay around Herself. Sure and she scares me more than Big Deirdre, and I'm mortal afraid of her, I am so!'

'We'll protect you, O'Liam,' I assured him.

'And who will protect you, Lady?' he muttered. 'Sure and didn't you get clapped in an iron cage the last time you met Big Deirdre, and had it not been for me you'd be there still – or worse!'

'True,' I admitted, 'but last time she caught us unawares. This time, we've got the drop on her.'

'We have?' Gwydion asked.

'Well, of course we have. She's in there consoling her heartbroken chum the Bog Fairy. We sneak in, shape-shift and freeze her so she has to listen to us.'

'Can't we just go in, get T.A. and leg it?' Gwydion asked.

'We could, but the more I think about it, the more I think Big Deirdre would be a good person to have on our side. One scary thing less to worry about if she's with us. And whatever else you say about Big Deirdre, you can't say she's at all fond of leprechauns – especially Conor!'

'And me,' muttered O'Liam.

'But you aren't Conor's any longer,' I pointed out. 'You've sworn fealty to Gwydion Dragonking, right?'

O'Liam didn't look either comforted or convinced.

I softened. 'Oh, all right. You stay out here with Elffin. Gwydion and I will go in. And don't worry. We'll be fine.'

I wished I felt as confident as I sounded. Elffin and O'Liam tucked themselves back into hiding while Gwydion and I shifted into a pair of mice and scuttled back into the cottage. Cornelia had put away her hanky and was munching on an oatcake and a huge slab of cheese. Maybe food cured blighted love.

Gwydion and I huddled side by side. 'One, two, three, *shift!*' I said softly, and the air shimmered about us as we stretched up and out and into our own shapes.

Cornelia's mouth fell open, revealing a tragic set of misaligned choppers and some half-chewed cheese, a bit like a cemetery full of old tombstones covered in lumpy custard. Not a pretty sight, believe me. Big Deirdre almost dropped her teapot.

Fast as I could, I zapped the pair of them with a spell that froze them. They could see, hear and breathe, but moving was out of the question. Cornelia's eyes were wide as car headlamps, but a lot more panic-stricken. Big Deirdre's were narrowed in fury at a witch being in her little cottage and she not able to do a thing about it. Gwydion set about untying T.A.

'Sorry to have to do that to you,' I said, 'but we need you to hear what we have to say. I know you don't like me, and it's your job to guard your port against alien incomers, but if you listen, I think you'll agree that we have a common enemy.'

Big Deirdre's eyes were still narrowed distrustfully, but she was listening. She had to.

'Conor of the Land Beneath hunted down your baby, Big Deirdre, and killed it. I know this is true, because I've seen what he did to your cub. It was the worst thing I've ever seen in my life. Nobody, not even a Leprechaun King should be allowed to do that to anyone. Nothing brave about killing a baby giant. It was cruel and cowardly.'

Big Deirdre's eyes filled with tears that slowly spilled over, dripped off her chin and plopped on her clean pinny.

'Conor of the Land Beneath and the Spiderwitch – Merch Corryn Du we call her – have ganged together. They are going to attack the Island of Summer. They want to rule it, and then the two of them plan to rule Erin, too.'

Big Deirdre was listening now. Intently.

'But both you and I know that the Spiderwitch is ten times stronger than Conor. Once she's taken Ynys Haf, do you think she will allow him to live, let alone rule?'

I had her full attention.

'No. As soon as she's captured both lands, there will be only one ruler. Do you want to be ruled by Spiderwitch?'

I unfroze her head so she could answer.

'I do not. Better the devil I know, and Conor of the Land Beneath is the devil I know best. And Conor will die, you may count upon it, for what he did to my poor wee babby.'

Cornelia was coming round, her eyes revolving in her head.

'So, Big Deirdre. Will you help us defeat Spiderwitch?'

'I will so,' said Big Deirdre. 'I will consult my friends and my comrades, and perhaps we shall help you defeat the Spiderwitch. But if we do, afterwards, Conor of the Land Beneath is mine.'

'Agreed,' I said firmly. Then I had a thought. 'Friends and comrades?' I asked, not at all sure I wanted to hear the reply.

'Aye. The Pwca Horse, the Great Worm of Mullingar, the Terrible Beast of Loch Ree – and one or two more besides should I decide to involve them. To defeat Spiderwitch, we shall need all the help we can get.'

I gulped. 'Does that include the Banshee?' I wasn't too eager to meet up with her again.

'Ah, now that poor soul may not be able to help us at all. Terrible toothache she has, so. Ate some sweeties a while back that were the best she'd ever tasted. Isn't she eating everything with sugar in it as fast as she's able ever since? Rotted every tooth in her head, she has, and her figure's a sight more substantial than it was, also.' Big Deirdre shook her head sadly. 'Totally affected her disposition, it has. Toothache will do that to a banshee.'

I felt slightly guilty. It was me who gave her a taste for treacle toffee . . .

T.A., rubbing her wrists, stood beside me. 'Thanks, Tanz,' she said, grinning. 'I knew you'd rescue me.'

I gave her a frown. 'It would have been really nice if I hadn't had to, T.A.,' I said reprovingly. 'I've got other things on my plate.'

'Yes, but now Big Deirdre is on our side – by the way, had you better unfreeze her?'

I'd forgotten about that. I unfroze the two of them, and the Bog Fairy promptly fainted again.

Big Deirdre's lip curled. 'She's no stamina, that one,' she announced. 'No stamina at all. That's what falling in love does to a woman. And speaking of love, is the O'Liam with you?'

'Yes,' I admitted.

'Then keep him well away from herself,' Big Deirdre advised, 'for she's as lorn and torn as a loony about him, she is so. She'll be no good at all in any sort of a battle. I'll send her home first, out of the way.' She eyed Gwydion, tall beside me. 'Mind,' she said, batting her eyelashes at him, 'I can understand the love thing a bit when I look at himself standing there. Keep your eye close on him, Lady of Ynys Haf, or someone may steal him away from you, so they might!'

Gwydion winced. I grinned up at him. 'Oh, I will,' I said. 'I wouldn't want him stolen.'

'Now,' Big Deirdre said, 'I'll send Cornelia home to her bog and then we'll make plans.' She crossed to where the Bog Fairy slumped in her chair, her mouth still open, and began patting her face to bring her round.

Suddenly the door burst open and O'Liam and

Elffin burst in. Lucky for them we'd already sorted the Big Deirdre problem.

'Will you be quick!' O'Liam panted. 'Move yourself this instant, for hasn't a mighty swarm of wasps just passed overhead like the devil's emissaries! Spiderwitch and Conor are on the move!'

And on their way to invade Ynys Haf.

13

I could see the black swarm out over the sea like an ominous, deadly cloud against the horizon. We had to get back quickly, and hope Gwyddno could reach Ynys Haf unmolested. What if the wasps saw his boat and attacked him? He would certainly die, stung by so many wasps. Then I remembered that he couldn't die of anything other than drowning in Cantre'r Gwaelod . . . All the same, I was sure they would somehow prevent him from reaching Ynys Haf if they saw him.

Panic-stricken, I stared at Gwydion, frantically trying to make my brain work. What could we do? We had to be something faster than wasps. But what?

'Dolphins!' I said, my brain suddenly unfreezing. I sprinted for the beach. 'Come on! Move!'

T.A., Gwydion, O'Liam and Elffin were hard on my heels, but we left Big Deirdre behind to keep an eye on events in Erin. As soon as we reached the incoming tide, we waded out and I shifted everyone who couldn't shift themselves. Then six bottle-nose dolphins set off in the direction of Ynys Haf, swimming as if our entire lives depended on it (which they did). We flashed like arrows through the clear water, cutting through schools of fish, and on the way picking up a family of genuine dolphins who decided to join in the fun. Half way across the Middlesome Sea I arched into the air and saw – behind us, thank goodness – a vast black buzzing swarm. We'd overtaken them, but they were still close and the unaccustomed swimming was taking its toll of all of us – except the real dolphins, who were leaping out of the water scattering clouds of rainbow spray and thoroughly enjoying themselves. Then I had an idea. I flung myself upward into the air, and turned into a gull. I sped along at wave-top height in front of the wasps, mentally flipping over the pages of the Lady's book of natural magic. I knew there was a wind spell somewhere – ah, yes! I squawked the spell in the face of the advancing swarm. At once a cold breeze sprang up. I folded my wings and dived, changing back into a dolphin as I hit the surface and hurtling after the others. The wind would blow into the wasps' wings and delay them, give us time to reach Ynys Haf and raise the alarm. A little further on I spotted the shape of a fishing boat bobbing above us. Heading for the surface I arched out of the water, spotted Gwyddno on board (looking definitely greenish) and dived again – straight at the deck, which almost gave the sailors a heart attack, since they all scattered and ducked. I shifted before I landed, which gave them another bit of a turn, landed lightly on deck, and grinned at them. Then I turned my attention to Gwyddno.

'Conor and Spiderwitch are on their way to Ynys Haf – there's a swarm of wasps the size of the Millennium Stadium about half a mile behind us. You have to come with me.'

Gwyddno opened and shut his mouth, then shrugged, as if to say 'oh, go on then.' I shoved him off the boat and shifted him into a dolphin before he started to drown, and we set off after the others.

With the wind delaying the wasps, and we dolphins swimming as if a great white shark were on our tails, we reached Yys Haf in record time. Once on shore I shifted us into merlins, and we headed for Cantre'r Gwaelod to warn them. We left Gwyddno Garanhir there to oversee his own defences, and then headed for Castell Du.

We landed in the courtyard, and I was gratified to see Branwen come hurtling out of one of the towers to meet us as we shifted. She tried to curtsy to Gwydion and me before she stopped running and almost fell on her nose. Her eyes shone with excitement.

'Oh, Lady, you're back!' she stammered, hopping from foot to foot.

'We are indeed,' I said, shifting O'Liam, T.A. and Elffin, who had decided to stay with us and let his father cope with any attack on Cantre'r Gwaelod. I think there was an element of 'old wolf, young cub' involved. Elffin was just old enough not to enjoy taking orders from his Dad – especially in front of T.A., apparently!

I was about to start shrieking at messengers when Gwydion took over.

Cupping his hands about his mouth he filled his lungs and bellowed at the guards on top of the tower. 'Guards! Light the beacons! Quickly! We're under attack!'

Two men-at-arms came running from opposite ends of the battlements, hurtling towards a metal basket on a stand. They crashed into each other, staggered, recovered, found flint and straw, dropped the flint, picked it up, struck a spark, lit the straw, blew on it, and applied it to the stuff in the metal basket. It caught immediately, blazing orange against the sinking sun, sending a plume of black smoke into the sky. In a matter of minutes, on the horizon in all directions similar leaps of flame and plumes of smoke streamed upward, as the warning of attack went from end to end of Ynys Haf as each beacon was lit and spotted.

'When did you set that up?' I demanded. 'Shows remarkable forethought, considering!'

'Considering what, exactly?' Gwydion said, sounding a little miffed. 'I did it as soon as I knew we were likely to have problems. I *am* Dragonking, you know. All these beacons were stowed away in the cellars, so I just set them up and made the men-at-arms practise lighting them.' He grinned. 'I think they could have done with a bit more of it, don't you?'

A languid voice spoke behind us. 'It would have been far quicker to have simply lit them by magic, Dragonking. But then, thinking was never your strong point.'

We swung round. 'Merlin!' Gwydion yelled. 'About blooming time!'

Merlin shrugged. I was so used to seeing him in jeans and a joky t-shirt that it was a bit of a shock to see him soberly dressed in a long robe like a monk's habit. 'I can't be everywhere, my boy. I came when I could. I'm horrified at what you have allowed to happen to Ynys Haf in my absence. I shall have to work extremely hard to put this right.'

I expected Gwydion to say, 'Sorry, Merlin Sir, won't do it again, Sir,' something like that, but he surprised me.

'Then you'd better get on and fix it, hadn't you?' he said coldly. 'That's your job. If you hadn't been off interfering with Arthur and Gwenhwyfar, and had been here where you're supposed to be, instead, perhaps it might not be in such a state. And in my opinion it was remarkably irresponsible of you, as Chief Wizard of Ynys Haf, to switch off your aura and be unreachable at a time of crisis. And I'll thank you to remember that I am the High Dragonking of Ynys Haf, and not "your boy"!'

Then I expected Merlin to swat Gwydion like a fly. But to my surprise his face went still with surprise, and then – there was *almost* a twinkle in his eyes. 'I take your point,' the Wizard admitted. 'Perhaps we should both be about our own tasks, yes?'

'Yes indeed.' Gwydion's voice was calm. 'I have a battle to fight, and you have a land to heal.' He turned his back and began to bark orders, summoning guards and putting the castle on battle status. Merlin silently turned on his pointy shoes and returned to his turret.

To my amazement, as soon as Merlin was inside the tower, Gwydion's knees buckled. I grabbed his arm to steady him.

'Gwydion! What's the matter? Are you ill?'

'Ill? No, just scared witless! That's the first time I've ever stood up to Merlin. That was scary, Tanz!'

I grinned, and an answering smile broke through. 'It won't be the last, Gwyd. Better get used to it, I s'pose!'

Unthinkingly, we gave each other a delighted, smacking kiss and hug and then realised we were doing it in front of the castle's assembled army. Several tough men-at-arms were grinning soppily at the sight of their Dragonking and the Lady having a bit of a snog . . .

'Um!' I said, scowling fiercely over his shoulder. 'Should one of us be at Castell y Ddraig, Dragonking?'

He let me go, quick. 'No. We stay together. If they get past us then Ynys Haf is lost. We stay together and we try to fight Conor of the Land Beneath with our magic. But we need Flissy and Nest beside us. How can we fetch them?'

'Perhaps they'll see the beacons and come anyway,' I suggested. Then I had a better idea. 'Branwen!' I bellowed, and a small titian-haired figure shot out of a doorway.

'Yes, Lady?' she panted. 'I'm all ready to seckertise.'

I hid a grin. 'Don't need a secretary right now, *cariad*,' I assured her. 'What I need is a messenger.'

'Shall I get Gronow Swiftfoot?' she said, blushing at being called a little sweetheart in front of everybody.

'Nope. I'm sending you. You have to get to the *tŷ hir* and fetch Flissy and Nest. Can you do that?'

''Course I can, Lady! But it'll take me ever so long . . .'

'No it won't.' I shifted the child into a bright-eyed merlin and popped her on my shoulder while I hastily scribbled a note for her to carry round her leg. 'Good luck!' I yelled, hurling her into the air. Even if she didn't reach Flissy and Nest in time, at least she'd be safely away from here.

Her small, sickle-shaped wings rowed the air, and the brown-backed, speckle-fronted bird flew like the wind towards towards the *tŷ hir*.

Gwydion had finished giving orders and was up on

the battlements. I ran up the steps to join him. Out to sea, a large dark cloud was approaching . . .

'They're coming!' he muttered. 'I wonder how they'll attack.'

I wondered if they would attack us as wasps. I didn't think I could cope with that. I've been stung twice by wasps and the closest thing I could relate it to was being stuck with a red hot needle. I made such a fuss that Mam took jam sandwiches off the menu, and kept a wasp trap outside the kitchen door every summer from then on –

'Gwydion!' I yelped. 'I've got an idea!'

The Lady's book had no handy spells for what I had in mind. I had to improvise, this time, sort of cut and paste. I shut my eyes, shuffled through a couple of likely incantations, and then opened them very wide and concentrated on the beach below us. It began slowly, and then quicker as I got the feel for combining three spells at once.

First, I put a solid wall of strawberry jam sandwiches along the tideline. Very little bread, but lots of sweet, sticky, ooooozy red jam.

A few metres behind that, I put a long row of open wine bottles half-filled with mead – alcoholic honey drink, classic wasp trap.

A few metres behind the bottles, I poured a thick lake of treacle, two metres wide and a couple of centimetres thick, right along the sea-shore.

Lastly, I magicked myself the biggest aerosol of wasp zapper I could possibly hold, (and yes, I know that was cheating, but this was self-defence!) and stood ready to do battle.

'Jam sandwiches?' Gwydion said unbelievingly. 'Bottles of mead? What good do you think they're going to do??'

'You've obviously never had a picnic on the Gower in summer, Gwyd,' I said feelingly. 'Beaches and wasps go together like fish and chips, trust me. Just wait and see!'

We waited, and the black cloud got nearer and nearer, and more and more sinister. Even though they were perhaps a hundred metres out to sea, we could hear their high, irritating buzzing. Made my skin crawl, to be honest.

The first wave of wasps crossed the tideline and reached the defensive line of jam sandwiches. These were only leprechauns *magicked* into wasps, remember. Not real wasps. As leprechauns, they didn't have the strength to resist the wasp nature. They swooped onto the jam sandwiches as if they'd been magnetised. Within seconds the sandwiches were completely hidden under a mass of squirming bodies.

The next wave flew over, and came to the mead. Once again, the trap worked. Ten thousand wasps flew down a thousand bottlenecks – and couldn't get out again. The air was loud with their frantic buzzing, but that was a few more of the enemy nobbled.

Then the cloud of wasps (somewhat smaller!) reached the puddle of treacle. They were on it like nobody's business, and of course their nasty little legs got stuck. That put paid to a few more.

But there were still more wasps, thousands of them, and they were heading for us. I raised my aerosol and got ready to squirt.

14

The cloud of wasps suddenly formed itself into a tight coil. It reared over Castell Ddu like some monstrous, buzzing tornado, and T.A., Elffin, O'Liam, Gwydion and I stared at it in horror. If the wasps attacked, we'd be helpless, stung to death before we could move. There were still just too many of them.

Two large wasps detached themselves from the column and flew earthward. They landed on the opposite side of the moat, and in a shimmer of air transformed into Conor of the Land Beneath and Merch Corryn Du. Whatever they were planning for the wasp-leprechauns, Conor and Spiderwitch obviously intended keeping their precious selves safe.

The swarm hovering above us twitched, and I knew they were about to attack. Suddenly my brain, half-paralysed with terror, got moving, and I shouted out a spell as loudly as I could. A vast, transparent dome appeared between the swarm and the castle, and slid silently downward, completely enclosing us. In the sudden silence I heard Gwydion say, 'Well done, Tanz!'

'Don't mention it,' I said fervently. 'I'd have done it sooner only my brain wasn't working. I think it was sort of frozen with terror!'

'M-mine, too!' T.A. stammered, and Elffin and O'Liam looked a bit pale around the gills.

The tiny wasp-bodies battered themselves against the shimmering dome, slid off and down its sides, regrouped and tried again.

Spiderwitch, below, was waving her arms in fury, and Conor's face was a tight mask of anger.

'It isn't going to last forever, though,' I said. 'Sooner or later Spiderwitch is going to make it disappear. And then we've got trouble.'

'What can we do?' Gwydion asked. 'I can't think of anything that will let us get past a swarm of wasps the size of that one.'

'Unless they aren't wasps,' T.A. suggested. 'Can you undo another witch's shape-shifts, Tanz?'

I shrugged. 'Dunno. Never tried. It's possible. I'll give it a go. Shape shifts are fairly easy magic.' I concentrated hard on a pair of wasps crawling on the clear canopy. I muttered the un-shifting spell, and added a twiddly-bit for luck. Suddenly the two wasps changed into panic-stricken leprechauns, clutching unsuccessfully at smooth, curved glass and slithering down, their mouths open in silent screams. 'Yes,' I said. 'I can.' So I did it a lot more, and watched a lot more leprechauns slithering to earth at a rate that people at Oakwood pay hard cash to enjoy! Gwydion soon got the hang of it, and before long we were shifting the leprechauns in dozens, then fifties, then hundreds, and soon there were only half a dozen terrified leprechauns clinging on to the canopy with their eyes shut.

Down below, however, there was an army of bad-tempered small golden people, and Spiderwitch was arming them with various sharp and heavy implements that she was producing from thin air. When every leprechaun was bristling with pointy swords and spears and stuff, Spiderwitch turned her attention to the dome. It was beginning to go cloudy in places, and I knew it wouldn't be long before it melted away altogether.

'They're going to attack us,' I said bleakly. 'And although we can hold out for a bit, there's no way we can beat them. Even though we've got rid of some of them, there are still thousands of them compared to us. Our people are too widely scattered. They'll never get here in time. I think we've lost, Gwydion.'

Just as the last of the transparent dome melted away, two black-backed gulls arrowed down onto the battlements, shimmered and changed into Flissy and Nest.

'Thank goodness you're here,' I said, 'but where's Branwen?'

'She had an idea,' Flissy said, sticking her nose over the battlements to see the gathering throng of angry leprechauns below. 'She said she'd see us later.'

'I hope she stays away,' I said miserably. 'I don't think we can beat all these, even with all of us here, and all our combined magic. I don't want anything to happen to her. I'm a failure, Fliss!'

'Nonsense,' Flissy said crossly. 'You're the Lady. Gwydion's Dragonking. I'm a Moonwitch, one of the original Circle of Seven. Of course we can beat them. They're only Conor's minions. They don't have nearly as much magic, all of them together, as we have. Positive thinking, Tan'ith, that's what we need.'

'Right, positive thinking,' I said glumly.

'It would be useful if Merlin were here, however,' Nest said. 'And Taliesin would be a help, too.'

'Merlin *is* here,' I said. 'But I don't know how

much help he's going to be. He's concentrating on healing Ynys Haf. He isn't remotely interested in saving *us*. And besides, Gwydion just told him off. I think he's probably sulking.'

Gwydion looked guilty.

'Gwydion *what?'* Fliss and Nest said together.

'I answered him back,' Gwydion said glumly. 'He was trying to put me in my place, like he did when I was a little apprentice magician, and I decided I'm too big to put up with it any more. So I sort of told him where to get off.'

'He did,' I affirmed, nodding vigorously. 'He really, really did. It was great. Maybe not particularly wise, but great for all that.'

'If you lived to tell the tale, Gwydion dear, and you're still in the same shape you started the day in, then Merlin probably realised that you were right,' Nest said briskly. 'Now if I'm not mistaken, my little golden relatives down there are about to attack. Flissy, I think you'd better talk to Merlin.'

Flissy nodded. 'Where is he, Tanz? In his tower?'

'I think so. But I don't think he'll help us.'

There was a loud angry roar from below us, and the clatter and clang of swords battering shields. Then the sound of two thousand running feet, and a thousand warlike leprechauns flung themselves at the castle walls. I thought briefly of summoning the bee colonies from all over Ynys Haf, but although I knew they would gladly die for me and Gwydion, I couldn't bring myself ask them to use their one precious, suicidal sting to save us. There were plenty of wasps in Ynys Haf, but wasps were unpredictable, and nasty creatures, and there was a chance that Spiderwitch might be able to turn them against us, too.

Then Elffin, who was busily buckling on body armour that Gwydion had magicked for everyone, shouted and pointed.

I wondered if somehow Gwyddno Garanhir had miraculously managed to gather his army and come like the cavalry in a cowboy film, to save us. He'd have had to move at the speed of light if he had, the distance Cantre'r Gwaelod was away from us. So what was Elffin getting excited about? I followed his pointing finger, squinting into the coppery sunshine. Something huge was flapping towards us. Something huge and red.

'Bugsy!' Gwydion and I shrieked together. I leapt up and down and waved my arms, and the dragon increased speed, zooming towards us like a vast red fighter plane. He circled the castle once, twice, and then sent a blast of flame earthwards, frizzling several attacking leprechauns, sending the rest running for their lives, and badly scorching the castle walls.

'Come back, you cowards!' Conor shrieked after his fleeing army, 'I command you to come back!'

Bugsy took a deep breath and a lick of fire scuttled along the ground towards Conor, who decided that discretion was the better part of valour and dodged behind a tree. Spiderwitch stood her ground, but when Bugsy swooped down on her with a large talon extended in her direction she dodged back quickly, shimmered, and disappeared.

'Damnation!' I said. 'She's got away!'

Conor was running in frantic circles around his tree,

and Bugsy appeared to be playing with him the way a cat plays with a mouse. Suddenly Conor disappeared, and the dragon turned his attention to a few straggling leprechauns who weren't leaving as quickly as he thought they should. When the last little golden man had abandoned his weapons and headed for safety, Bugsy gathered himself under his wings and set off for home. He did a victory roll over the castle first, though!

Something perched on my shoulder and gently nibbled my ear. 'Hello, Branwen,' I said, lifting her down, setting her on the stone flags and shape-shifting her. 'Well done, you saved our bacon. I couldn't have done better myself.'

Her freckles went crimson with delight. 'I was afraid we wouldn't be in time, Lady.'

'Well, you were. You've given us a chance to regroup.'

'Do you think they'll attack again, then?' T.A. asked.

'I don't think we'll see the mini-minions again,' Gwydion replied, 'but Spiderwitch and Conor won't give up so easily. There's too much at stake. But now we have a chance. We've at least won some time to prepare.'

'I'm going to have words with Merlin,' Flissy said firmly. 'He needs a good talking-to, that man.'

'And you're just the person to give it to him,' Gwydion muttered, grinning.

'He's acted thoroughly irresponsibly for far too long,' Flissy scowled. 'Swanning off to play around with Arthur and Gwenhwyfar and that rackety

Camelot crowd. Time he settled down and got on with the job in this Time, not messing around all over the When.' She rolled up her sleeves (or should that be Rolled Up Her Sleeves?) and marched down the spiral staircase into the courtyard. I watched her emerge, cross the octagonal space, and start determinedly up the spiral staircase to Merlin's tower.

'Now there'll be fireworks!' T.A. said.

'Probably,' Gwydion agreed. 'But that's for them to sort out. We've got Spiderwitch and Conor running around loose, and there are about eight hundred assorted leprechauns pootling about Ynys Haf as well. What are we going to do about them?'

'The best thing to do would be to round them up, I suppose,' T.A. said thoughtfully.

'Round them up? What with? Sheepdogs?' I asked.

'Sort of.'

'We haven't got that many sheepdogs, T.A.'

'No, but we've still got the Oldway Creatures, haven't we?'

Light dawned. The Oldways were still lurking in Bugsy's mountain refuge like overgrown puppies. They'd be wonderful at tracking down the leprechauns and penning them in one place. Iestyn, with his 'headman of the village' hat on, could organise people to ride them and a place to keep the leprechauns once they'd been captured. They'd have to be a bit careful of the small amounts of magic the leprechauns had – all of them had sufficient to make them thoroughly sneaky, if nothing else. However, if we could remove the remnants of Conor's army and tuck it away somewhere safe, then we could fight on more equal terms. I felt a lot safer using magic than I did using brute strength and sticking sharp bits of metal into people. I wasn't keen on the blood stuff – especially when some of it might be mine!

Nest volunteered to fly to the village and get Iestyn to organise the Oldway Creature patrols, Gwydion and Elffin went to order a careful watch over the surrounding countryside and out to sea, and T.A. and I went in search of Flissy.

Merlin was in his tower, his face thunderous. Flissy stood, arms folded, with her back to the door.

'And another thing,' she was saying, 'don't you dare switch off your aura again while you and Taliesin are off gallivanting! That could have caused all sorts of problems. Where were you when Ynys Haf needed you? This poor country is dying of thirst, and do you care? No, you don't. You're quick enough to accuse Gwydion of being lackadaisical and useless, but that boy has kept this country together in your absence. You don't give him credit for the brains he's got. And Tan'ith, too. She's been trying her very best to cope with all sorts of things. She may be the Lady, but don't forget she's half mortal and comparatively new to all this.'

Merlin muttered something.

'Speak up!' Flissy ordered.

'I said, that's his job, isn't it? And she's got to learn. If she has to learn on the job, that's not my problem.'

'You are supposed to be here to support both of them. That's in the contract, isn't it?'

Merlin growled something that sounded rather like

130

"Oh, *!#@+?> the =[$£@<~# contract!", but when Flissy raised one eyebrow, he subsided.

'Oh, I suppose so,' he admitted at last. 'Anyway, I'm back now. Taliesin will be here any time, and I'd like to get started on sorting out this wretched weather if only you'd leave me in peace. And what are you doing here?' he bellowed, taking his frustrations out on me.

Emboldened by the way Gwydion had stood up to him, I folded my arms in imitation of Flissy. 'I don't know what this contract Flissy mentioned is all about, Merlin, but I agree with her anyway. I am the Lady, and I know that my task is to help Gwydion and listen when Ynys Haf talks to me. Ynys Haf is talking now, Merlin, and She's not happy!'

'Oh, good grief!' Merlin said, and disappeared in a puff of smoke.

15

'That's torn it!' I said miserably. 'He's gone off in a huff. I bet he won't come back.'

'Oh yes, he will,' Flissy said. A little smile lurked around the corners of her mouth. 'Trust me. He only ever disappears like that when he knows he's in the wrong. He's gone away to think about it, find a way of saving face, and then he'll be back. He'll act as if nothing at all has been said, but by the time he gets back he'll have sorted out some sort of a plan.'

I wished I felt as confident. But then, Fliss had known him years longer than I had – about a thousand, I think.

We trudged back down the stairs to the courtyard, where Gwydion and Elffin were issuing orders left, right and centre, sending men-at-arms all over the castle with orders to keep their eyes open. Flissy bustled off to get the castle kitchens organised into providing some food. When it came, great golden loaves of bread and wheels of cheese, we sat round a large table and munched while we made plans.

'I think I'd better go back to Cantre'r Gwaelod,' Elffin said glumly. 'Dada will need me, and I know my Mam won't be happy until she sees me in the flesh and knows I'm safe.'

'You're probably right,' I said, reaching for the knife to cut another hunk of fresh bread off the loaf.

'But –' T.A. said, and then shut up.

I knew what she was thinking. She had a great, big, soft spot for Elffin. The trouble was, I knew what was going to happen to him in Cantre'r Gwaelod, and I didn't particularly want her to get involved with him. It's a bit of a dilemma, really, knowing that a bloke your best friend fancies something rotten is eventually going to get drowned.

'There's no point in you coming with me, T.A.,' Elffin said quietly. He picked up her hand and dropped a light kiss in the palm. T.A. went pink. 'I'll be back as soon as I possibly can. But I think I should be at my father's side if Spiderwitch and Conor are going to attack. And they're as likely to attack Cantre'r Gwaelod as anywhere.'

'I don't think so,' I said thoughtfully. 'I think they'll come for Gwydion and me, first. Probably their plan is to just move in and then take over the rest of Ynys Haf as a next stage. I think T.A. might probably be safer with you than she would here.'

T.A. looked from one to the other of us. 'Don't ask me what I want to do, will you?' she said indignantly. 'Oh no, not me. I'm just a piece of furniture you can shift around until you find a place where I look good!'

'Oh, for goodness sake, T.A!' She was beginning to exasperate me. 'Do what you want. Stay with us, go with Elffin. I'm only the Lady here. Nobody takes any notice of what I think!'

'You may be the Lady, Tanz, but you're still my best friend!' she yelled. 'And you can be a real pain, sometimes!'

'So can you!' I yelled back. Then our eyes met and we both collapsed in giggles. It was usually like that when we argued. I think a good shout helped to ease the tension anyway. It had been a fairly fraught day.

Once we'd calmed down, we made plans.

'We can't hang about here waiting for Spiderwitch and Conor to attack again,' I said. 'Being inside Castell Du feels safe, but it isn't. If we were being attacked by ordinary armies we could keep them out for ever, no problem. But Spiderwitch's magic could get her inside and among us and then we'd be in trouble. She could zap us all before we even knew she was around. We have to get out and find them. Take the battle to them before they expect us.'

'You think they won't be expecting us?' Gwydion asked grimly. 'Whyever not?'

'Oh,' I grinned wickedly, 'they'll be expecting us all right. They just won't know what as, or when. It's better that way. Our chief weapon is –'

'Surprise!' T.A. and I chorused together,

'– and fear!' I bellowed, then we both collapsed in hoots and snorts of laughter while Gwydion, Elffin and O'Liam stared, mystified.

'Sorry,' I said, wiping my eyes. 'Old Monty Python sketches. Spanish Inquisition. You wouldn't understand.'

O'Liam had sneaked the last piece of cheese while we were otherwise engaged. He looked up at Gwydion. 'When your man goes home to Cantre'r Gwaelod, would it be all right with yourself if I went with him, Dragonking?' He put a large lump of bread in his mouth and gazed at Gwydion anxiously. 'Only it's a fair wee while since I saw Siobhan Flowerface, and with a wedding coming up I feel I should at least try to get to know the dear thing before we are both entirely too old.'

'Go, O'Liam. Don't worry. We'll be dancing at your wedding before you can say Jack Robinson.'

'Now why would I say any such thing? I don't know the man at all.'

'Oh, never mind,' Gwydion said. 'I'll introduce you some time.'

The day ended with Elffin and O'Liam riding off into the sunset and T.A. staying behind. She'd thought about it, and had seen the sense of the two of us staying together. Once Elffin had gone, however, she sniffled a bit.

'Cheer up,' I said, punching her on the arm. 'It isn't the end of the world.'

'It might be,' she said miserably. 'We could both get splatted in the next twenty-four hours. Elffin might get waylaid on the way home and I might never see him again. There's not a lot of security in this Time, is there, Tanz?'

'There isn't much more in ours, if you think about it,' I said. 'Wars, people starving, terrorists flying planes into buildings. Not a lot has changed over the centuries, has it?'

'Except the magic somehow got lost along the way,' she said.

'Not all of it,' I reminded her. 'People like us still have the Power.'

But it was late, and we had to get some rest before we went hunting Spiderwitch. Surprisingly, I slept quite well – probably the excitement of the day had worn me out. There were plenty of guards on duty all night, but all the same Flissy and I carefully wrapped the castle in the strongest magic we could summon between us. It might not stop a witch as powerful as Merch Corryn Du getting *in* – but, like a piece of string attached to the doorknob at one end and your big toe at the other, it would certainly give us early warning!

But we slept peacefully, and woke to another fiendishly hot day. By eight o'clock the sun was hot enough to cook Welsh cakes on the flagstones in the courtyard, and even in the deep shade of the walls there was no relief. I'm a real sun-bunny – even though Mam makes me wear SPF three million if I stick my nose outdoors – and I love a hot day, especially if I'm by the sea. But this was different. The air was utterly still, and every movement brought clouds of fine dust puffing up from the ground which made everyone's eyes itch, and some of us with sensitive noses sneeze. To be honest, my nose has never recovered from Astarte Perkins putting a spell on it right at the beginning, just when I started to be a witch, and I sneezed until my nose was sore.

From Castell Du's battlements I should have been able to see a broad silver ribbon of river winding to the sea, but it had dried to a sluggish trickle, and the trees that should have been reflected in the water were dried, dead husks. The sea itself was as still as a millpond, not a whitecap or a ruffle disturbed its surface, and even the sea level seemed to be receding: a rim of white dried salt stained the beach below, and gulls sat miserably on the battlements, their beaks open to catch any oxygen that was going.

We ate breakfast, although for once I didn't feel at all like eating. Then Gwydion and I set off to search

136

for Spiderwitch and Conor of the Land Beneath. We decided to begin our search in the mountains near the cave that Bugsy had shown us. It was a reasonable bet that she'd head back to her lair, and that she'd probably insist that Conor went with her. Since neither of them trusted the other, it was unlikely that they'd let each other out of their sight!

There was a little relief in shifting into buzzards and soaring up into the heat-hammered sky. From below, we must have resembled giant moths – brown, cream and black wings upswept in a shallow 'V' shape, we coasted on windless air, the heat-haze shimmering below us, up into the amber, cloudless sky. Whatever Merlin planned to do to save Ynys Haf, he'd better do it quickly. The land was at death's door, and soon it would be altogether too late for recovery. Wales would be as dry as Death Valley, and the people would all starve. It would take centuries for the country to recover.

The air became marginally cooler when we reached the foothills of Snowdonia. The great peaks soared eerily ahead of us, and still we flew until we neared the place where Branwen had introduced us to Bugsy. The dragon was absent, and Gwydion soared over his peak in a broad sweeping circle looking for him, before swooping down to land. I glided in to perch beside him.

He ruffled his pale flight feathers over the dark coverts, and preened himself comfortable after the long flight. His bright black eyes surveyed me, then his outline shimmered and shifted. I stretched up and out, and took my own form. Even this high in the mountains the air was still, without any breath of wind.

'I think I should go into Spiderwitch's cave alone,' he said, wiping sweat from his forehead with the full sleeve of his shirt. 'That way, if anything happens to me, you can still get away.'

'Oh, sure,' I said sarcastically. 'Not on your life, Dragonking! We're in this together, matey. Where you go, I go. We're partners. Besides, nothing can happen to us. We're in the legends, right?'

'I'm beginning to think,' he said, staring at his dusty boots, 'that legends can be changed. For instance, while I was in your Time, I can't remember ever reading or hearing about a great drought that struck Ynys Haf. Can you?'

'Well, no –' I began.

'So this is something that has happened *out* of history somehow, right?'

'Not necessarily. It could have happened and no one wrote it down.'

'They wrote down Cantre'r Gwaelod, didn't they?'

'Well yes, but –'

'So it's unlikely that anything this serious would escape being written down.'

'Unless it didn't happen.'

'But it's happening, Tanz!' he said crossly. 'Look at it. It's like there's never been any rain, ever.'

'We had hot, dry summers in my Time, too, Gwyd. Nothing like this one, true. But if Merlin manages to mend Ynys Haf somehow before it dies entirely, maybe it was just remembered as a very dry period – and not written down. After all, no one has died yet.

Not like they did when Cantre'r Gwaelod was – I mean is – I mean, will be – flooded.' This Time business was getting confusing again.

He shrugged. 'Anyway, I still think I should go in alone.'

'And I said you shouldn't, remember? Absolutely not. No. Na. Nada. Non. Niente. Niet. Forget it, Gwyd. We go in together, or not at all.'

He sighed. 'And that's your last word?'

'It is.'

And then he zapped me. The rotten, lousy, sneaky pig clobbered me with a spell when I wasn't expecting it. I didn't think he could do that, but obviously some of the lessons he had from Merlin when he was a little kid had sunk in.

16

So there I was. Comprehensively zapped. The air went fuzzy, my eyes crossed, and my brain went missing. Sight, hearing, thought – all on temporary hold.

However, although he could apparently zap me, he couldn't keep me zapped. My eyes opened at last, onto a world bathed in pink sunset. One of those spells, then. The ones that only last until sunset, when my Moon takes over. Ha! I could have done better than *that*! I could have fixed Gwydion Rotten Dragonking so that he wouldn't have woken up *ever* – or at least until I was ready for him to. *If* I'd wanted to. But *I* wouldn't have done something as sneaky as that to *him*, oh no.

However, it would soon be dark, and he'd obviously been gone for hours and hours. I began to get that sinking feeling that sort of told me that, wherever Gwydion was, and whatever he'd been up to, he probably hadn't been too successful at it. The sun slithered down over the sea and the mountains turned blood-red, then purple, and then as black as the inside of a witch's wardrobe.

And my cowardy-custard bone started to twitch. Did I want to go Spiderwitch hunting in the pitch dark night? No way! Nowaynowaynoway.

Except that Gwydion was missing. Gwydion had gone to find Spiderwitch and hadn't come back. Did I want to wait until morning to find out what had happened to him?

Well, no. I didn't want to do that, either. If

Gwydion had got himself into trouble, I had to get him out of it, right? I sighed a great big sigh, shifted into tawny owl, blinked round me with large-ringed, dark eyes, and launched myself into the eerie night-world as seen through owl eyes. Tawny owls don't much like mountains, preferring woodland and farmland and nice thick protective forests, but this was an emergency. Halfway to Spiderwitch's cave I stooped on an unwary mouse and swallowed it head first, because it had been a long time since I'd eaten. The tail slithered down my throat like a piece of hairy spaghetti, and I felt much better. Seconds later I was on the wing again, and a short, silent flight brought me to the entrance to Spiderwitch's cave. I glided in to land and tucked myself into the rocks to listen. The night was absolutely still, and the only sound was the faint scratch of my talons on rock as I shifted and settled. Looked like Spiderwitch was sleeping or absent. But the question was, where was Gwydion?

Well, no use dithering about. I had to go and look. I arched my back, pushed my arms and legs outwards and shimmered into me-shape again. My shoulder muscles ached from unaccustomed flying, but at least the headache had gone.

I cautiously approached the cave entrance. The darkness was absolute – I walked smack into the ledge of rock and bashed my nose. Once my eyes stopped watering and I'd stopped swearing under my breath, I listened, just to make sure there was no movement inside. There wasn't – well, none that I could hear, anyway. I summoned the Moon, and it floated obediently overhead. It was so bright that I was a bit nervous about giving Spiderwitch advance warning that I was coming – if, that is, she was in there at all. So I turned down the brightness a bit, leaving a faint, comforting glow, just enough to stop me bumping into things and tripping over stuff.

The narrow passageway loomed ahead, the festoons of spiderwebs sagging horribly overhead, spiders of all shapes and sizes scuttling away from my approach and the bobbing light illuminating their dusty homes. Shuddering with horror, I brushed off a huge wolf spider that fell – or jumped, knowing wolf spiders – onto my shoulder, and I headed deeper into the cave. Every few yards I stopped and listened, but apart from my own breathing, there was no sound at all. Quite quickly (too quickly!) I came to the entrance to the huge inner cave. I slipped inside, cautiously, ready to run if something huge and spidery suddenly leapt out from somewhere. If Spiderwitch was about, she'd probably hear my heart galloping about in my chest like a herd of rhinoceros. I was so scared I couldn't breathe properly, and my whole body felt clammy. Why couldn't I be one of those brave, Joan of Arc types that go charging in waving a big sword or something? But then, look what happened to Joan of Arc . . . Barbecue City, right?

The huge spiderweb stretched up from the stalagmites. Great ropes of web glistened in the moonlight, globules of the sticky stuff gleaming horribly. I sent the Moon up to shine on the shadowy bits in the high roof of the cave, peering anxiously upwards, trying to see any bulky shapes wrapped round in web. Gwydion didn't seem to be there, and (hooray, hooray) neither did Spiderwitch. So, where were they? Did Spiderwitch have a second lair that we didn't know about?

Well, hanging about there waiting for Spiderwitch to come back and catch me didn't seem like a good way of finding out. So I (quite gratefully) turned on my heel and headed for the exit, the Moon bobbing a little way above my head. I made much faster time getting out than I had getting in. Cowardice really helps a person's speed!

Outside, my small Moon faded in the light of the real thing – huge and yellowish, surrounded by a reddish ring of haze, as if the dust from Ynys Haf had risen to pollute the skies as well as the land. I shifted back into owl shape and scouted around for a while looking for another cave, but there was nothing. I tried searching the slopes in the hope of finding Gwydion fast asleep somewhere, having a rest, but there wasn't a trace of him anywhere. So what else could I do? I went home.

I expected to find Castell Du in its early morning drowse, except for the men-at-arms patrolling the battlements and guarding the entrances. But even with the sun barely up, people were rushing about everywhere, and torchlight blazed in the Great Hall.

I swooped into the courtyard and shifted back, just in time to see Branwen hurtle out of a door, pigtails undone, glossy chestnut hair flying wildy about her face. I grabbed her arm and hauled her back as she ran past me.

'Branwen! Where's the fire?'

'Oh, Lady, thank goodness you're back! Oh, there's terrible things happening, Lady!'

My insides twisted. 'What? Where is everyone?'

'They're in the Magician's tower, Lady. They sent me to get breakfast took up to them, but the cook won't listen to me. She's packing all her stuff and says she's going home to her Mam.'

'We'll see about that! I stormed in through the archway and down the spiral stairs to the kitchen. The kitchen-maids were weeping and wailing, the scullery boy was hiding under the table, and the little turnspit dog (that I'd ABSOLUTELY FORBIDDEN when I'd discovered it!) was galloping panic-stricken in his little wheel although there was nothing on the spit for him to turn.

I stopped in the doorway and surveyed the chaos. 'RIGHT!' I thundered. 'WHAT is going on? Cook, when Branwen asks for food to be brought to Merlin's tower, food will be taken to Merlin's tower. Is that clear?'

Cook shoved the last of her voluminous bloomers into a cloth bag and straightened her hat. 'That's as may be, Lady,' she said mutinously, 'but there's no one in this world can make me stay here now I know what's going to happen.'

'What do you mean? What's going to happen?'

'We're all going to be murdered in our beds by that Spidery woman and that nasty little leprechaun from across the Middlesome Sea. Lot of hope there is for us if you don't even know,' she sniffed.

'I do know. And you're exaggerating. There's absolutely nothing to be afraid of.' (At this point I mentally crossed my fingers. And my toes and eyes and everything else crossable) 'In the meantime,

Cook, please have food taken up to Merlin's tower. Now. Or else.'

'Or else what, Lady?'

'You don't want to find out, Cook,' I said ominously, putting my nose very close to hers. 'You may be afraid of Merch Corryn Du, but I'm stronger than she is. When I'm disobeyed, I really get *quite cross*. Understand?'

Cook went white. 'Yes, Lady. I'll get some food ready now, Lady.' She unpinned her hat and reached for her pinny.

I opened the turnspit cage and lifted out the little dog. Its heart was thumping and it whined and licked my face. I tucked it under my arm. 'I told you that I wouldn't have turnspit dogs in this castle and I meant it. If I find you've got another one, then *you* will take its place. Forever. Understand? See how you like it.'

Cook went whiter. 'Yes, Lady. Sorry, Lady. Only, how do I stop the meat burning without no dog, Lady?'

'Turn it by hand. Get someone else to turn it. But no helpless little animals in that cage, right?'

She bobbed a shaky curtsy.

'I want food upstairs within fifteen minutes. And no more nonsense!'

I turned and marched out, followed by a pink-faced Branwen.

'Ooh, Lady, you told her!' she said gleefully.

The stairs to Merlin's tower twisted and turned. I started up them in fine, angry style, stamping up the grooved stone steps, the small, wriggling dog licking whichever bit of me he could reach, but halfway up I ran out of steam and had to slow down. By the time I got to the top and pushed open the door of Merlin's chamber, I had hardly any breath left to speak, and I was seeing stars.

Flissy, Nest and Merlin swung round as I tottered in. I handed the dog to Branwen, and he washed her face enthusiastically.

'Thank goodness you're back!' Flissy gasped. 'We were so worried about you!'

'I wasn't,' Merlin said coolly, slamming a huge book shut and releasing a cloud of dust into the atmosphere. 'I knew she was perfectly all right.'

'Well, good for you,' I said, sarcastically. I didn't care if he was the Great Magician of Ynys Haf. He had really teed me off, one way and another.

Merlin raised his eyebrows at my tone. 'What's chewing on your toenails?'

'I'd rather like to know what's going on. I've been up all night looking for Gwydion, and I can't find him anywhere. I come back to the Castle and everyone's running about like headless chickens. Cook has her hat on and is threatening to go home to her Mam, and I'm starving and Cook still hasn't done as she was told.'

I went to the door and bellowed down the stairs. 'Where's my breakfast?'

A faint voice echoed up from far below. 'Coming, Lady! Coming!'

Merlin opened another book. Something small and green with long scaly legs crawled out. He grabbed it by the tail and stuffed it back in between the pages rather like a bookmark. It seemed to dissolve into the parchment. 'Wretched spells getting above themselves.

That's the trouble with upheaval. It upheaves everything. Get one rogue witch wandering about making trouble and the whole system goes to pot,' he grumbled. 'It will take me ages to get things back to normal.'

'That's your job, isn't it?' I said icily. 'I thought Gwydion and I were going out to try to find Spiderwitch, and you and Taliesin were going to stay here and try to fix the weather.' I glanced out of the window, where the early morning sun was doing its best to melt the lead on the roof. 'Don't seem to have had much success yet, do you? Anyway, where's Taliesin?'

Merlin glared at me. 'Taliesin has taken off for Cantre'r Gwaelod. He's taken your mortal friend with him. And speaking of success, you don't seem to have had much yourself, do you?'

I was about to say something very sarcastic and horribly cutting, but suddenly realised that Aunty Fliss was screwing her dress up between her hands, something she only did when she was really worried, and Nest was watching Merlin and me with wide eyes, as if she was wondering which of us would self-destruct from temper first. I calmed down.

'I don't know where Gwydion is,' I said, sinking miserably down onto a bench. 'The wretch zapped me, and when I woke up he had gone. I looked for him in Spiderwitch's lair, but he wasn't there. I don't know where he is. He seems to have vanished.'

'As you so pointedly said,' Merlin commented snidely, reaching high up onto a shelf for an even dustier tome, 'that's not my problem. It's yours. I have Ynys Haf to consider.'

17

Couldn't argue with that, could I? But before I galloped off madly in all directions, I wanted my breakfast. When it came it was a bit of a disappointment, being bread and cheese and a nice, healthy drink of water. My teeth were all set for Full Welsh – but hold the laverbread and cockle fritters, I'm not too keen on those. So I magicked myself a proper Breakfast, and for Flissy, Nest and Branwen too: crispy bacon, fried egg, fried bread, mushrooms, tomatoes, beans – you name it, we had it. I deliberately didn't get one for Merlin. He didn't deserve it.

We sat at his table (first moving the stuffed hedgepig and the mouse cage) and tucked in. Merlin's nose was twitching, but his pride wouldn't let him either ask or magic the same for himself. Instead, he made do with the bread and cheese. Serves him right.

When we'd finished, I got rid of the mess and we sat with cups of hot tea and tried to think of a plan. The turnspit dog realised belatedly that there would be no more tasty bits coming his way, and went to sleep on Branwen's lap.

I sipped my tea and thought. And thought. The trouble was, where did we start to look? He could be anywhere. Fliss and Nest were just as stumped.

'The only thing to do is to scry for Gwydion, see if we can get a clue where he is and what he's doing,' I suggested at last.

Aunt Fliss found a wooden bowl and rinsed the dust out of it – Merlin's housekeeping left a lot to be desired. Then she took some leaves from the pouch hanging at her belt, dropped them in the bowl and set fire to them. The fragrant smoke rose and twisted round Merlin's tower before disappearing out of the window. When the fire was out, she filled the bowl with water and we peered into it. Branwen edged a bit closer to me. I think she was a bit nervous, not knowing much about magic. I put my arm round her, drew her towards the bowl, encouraged her to peer in. If she was going to be with me for long, she had to get used to it. Her little shoulders were tense and I gave her a reassuring squeeze.

Flissy blew gently across the surface of the bowl and the water rippled and became still. Branwen squeaked as, slowly, a picture formed: two people sitting at a huge, polished table, eating. It wasn't much of a Happy Meal: they weren't speaking to each other from the look of it. One was Conor of the Land Beneath, the other was Spiderwitch.

'Well,' I said, 'there're the baddies. Now, where's Gwydion?' I stirred the water with my forefinger, and waited until it stilled again.

But the scrying bowl wasn't showing us anything more than Conor and Spiderwitch. I looked again at the picture in the bowl, and drew my head back to get a wider picture. Sure enough the 'zoom lens' effect kicked in, and I was able to see the room. I recognised it instantly.

'They're in Conor's Great Hall in the Land Beneath!' I said miserably. 'And if they are there, maybe Gwydion is too.'

'Well, nothing's certain,' Fliss said, 'but since

Gwydion has disappeared, he's likely got himself into trouble, and since they're the only trouble in town or out, it's a pretty safe bet, I suppose. So, what next?'

'We go to the Land Beneath and look for him, I suppose. I just wish Gwydion hadn't gone off by himself. If I'd been with him he might have kept out of mischief.'

'Or both of you might have been captured,' Nest said reasonably.

We decided it would be best if Flissy stayed behind to take charge of Ynys Haf with Iestyn's help. Nest and I would fly to Cantre'r Gwaelod, and from there we'd head for Erin.

Nest and I shifted into peregrine falcons and headed for the coast. Gwyddno Garanhir's glorious land unrolled beneath us, acre after acre of what would have been (if not for the drought) rich fields of corn, orchards, silver rivers teeming with salmon, herds of deer, the sixteen towers of the sixteen cities of Cantre'r Gwaelod like pointing fingers. Taliesin's tower was the tallest, and as we flew past it the faint, barely-there breeze from the sea stirred the tinkling strings of seashells hanging in the windows.

We swooped in to land at Gwyddno's palace, and dropped into the courtyard. As we shimmered and shifted into ourselves, O'Liam came running, his pointed golden face lit up by our appearance.

'Is it yourself, Lady?' he asked. '*Dia daoibh.* Hello to you both!'

'Hi, O'Liam,' I said, brushing a feather off my breeches. 'How's Siobhan Flowerface and the courtship coming along?

The little man kissed his fingertips. 'Is she not the sun in my sky, Lady? Although –' he glanced skyward, '– perhaps rain might be entirely more useful at the minute.'

'And Maebh? How is she getting along?' Nest asked.

O'Liam's face darkened. 'Ah, isn't she driving the whole of the sixteen cities of Cantre'r Gwaelod insane with her wants and her needs and her tantrums! I am wholly amazed Lady Garanhir has not gone entirely mad yet, what with dealing with her day in, day out!'

'Where are T.A. and Elffin?' I looked around me, expecting to see them appear.

O'Liam laid a conspiratorial finger alongside his nose. 'Well you may ask. Are the two of them not out walking on the sea wall? Hand in hand and whispering sweet somethings?'

Oh, great. Just what I needed. My best mate getting seriously involved with someone who was about to get drowned. More complications. It was all right when they were just flirting, but holding hands and going for walks and stuff is *serious*, right? I was going to have to Speak to T.A.

Taliesin wandered into the courtyard. 'Oh, hi, Tanz, Nest. What are you doing here?'

'Guess,' I said shortly. 'Gwydion's gone missing, and Conor and Spiderwitch are back in the Land Beneath. We've got an idea that they may have Gwydion, so we're going to look for him. Are you coming?'

'Can't. Merlin sent a message this morning telling me to go and sort out some stuff for him in another Time. I'm off as soon as I've got myself organised.'

When O'Liam heard that Gwydion was missing, he insisted on coming to look for his Dragonking, even if it meant leaving Siobhan to travel back to Castell Du to get ready for the wedding. They took a tender leave of each other, with little kisses and sniffles.

Nest and I shifted into dolphins and headed out to sea, towing O'Liam behind in a little boat. There was no wind to speak of, and the sea was flat calm, and so for a change it was a comfortable ride for the leprechaun. Nest and I arrowed along under a surface like an inverted mirror, the sea as warm as milk, one of us occasionally leaping skyward for the fun of it, scattering rainbows of water droplets, splashing down and hurtling onward. We thought we might be safe going in at Big Deirdre's port this time – after all, she was on our side now, and I had had an idea for how to keep her on our side. I wasn't sure if it would work, but if it did – well, we'd see.

Once on shore, and shifted, we set off up the cliff path towards Big Deirdre's whitewashed cottage. It was strange to see a land that was green and healthy with meandering silver streams, after Ynys Haf's desert-like appearance. O'Liam decided it wouldn't be good for his health to visit Big Deirdre, just in case the Bog Fairy was visiting: he'd wait for us a little way up the trail. When we reached the cottage, smoke was drifting from the hole in the sod roof, and the usual livestock chomped enthusiastically on top as we knocked on the divided door. The top half swung open, and the giantess poked her head out.

'Is it yourselves again?' she asked. 'Will you come inside?'

'If it is not too much trouble,' Nest replied politely. 'Peace and plenty be upon you and all in this house.'

'And upon you also,' Big Deirdre replied. She tugged open the bottom half of the door and in we went. 'Are you hungry at all?' she enquired.

'We are not,' Nest answered. 'But I thank you for asking. Do you know what has happened?'

'I do not. My friend Cornelia the Bog Fairy let slip with some powerful rumours, but she has no news except what her mind imagines. Her living in the middle of a bog, you understand, there will not be much in the way of passers-by at all. Mind, did I not with my own eyes see a great cloud of wasps heading for the Land across the Middlesome Sea, and didn't I say to myself at the time, "That is not natural, no, not at all".' Big Deirdre nodded vigorously, and the hairs on her chin wagged.

'That cloud of wasps was Conor's army of leprechauns. They attacked Ynys Haf, but we managed to beat them off. But Conor and the Spiderwitch escaped, and Gwydion Dragonking and the Lady went to try to find them, but only the Lady came back. We don't know what has happened to our Dragonking,' Nest explained.

'Does the Lady not know?' Big Deirdre asked, puzzled.

'Nope. The Dragonking decided he'd be brave and go off on his own.'

Big Deirdre clucked her tongue. 'Isn't that just like a man, so! Do you not have an idea where he might be?'

'Conor may have him. He's come back here, and so has Spiderwitch.'

'And what can Deirdre, Guardian of the Port, do to help you? For we made a bargain, did we not? I should help you, and in your turn you would help me to take my revenge on Conor of the Land Beneath.'

'We did indeed,' I replied. 'What you can do to help us is to make sure that all the hazards that live around here leave us alone. We shall have enough to do with Conor and Spiderwitch, without worrying about stuff like Black Dogs and Pwca Horses and Banshees and such. Can you do that?'

'Oh, I can so. And in return?' She raised one quizzical eyebrow. It looked like a hairy caterpillar crawling up her forehead.

I took a deep breath. 'In return, you shall have the opportunity to take your revenge on Conor of the Land Beneath – that's assuming he survives whatever the Spiderwitch has in mind! I don't think their alliance will last too long.'

'If the Spiderwitch beats me to it and kills him dead first, then that will be that, so it will. However, could you not think of some other little tempty-bit to cheer me along? What else will you give me?'

'I will give you your heart's desire,' I said, crossing my fingers beneath the table and ignoring Nest's panicky look. I had an idea, you see. I didn't want to talk about it yet – but if it came off . . .

Big Deirdre looked sad. 'My heart's desire is not possible. Is not my wee babby dead at Conor's hands?'

'Wait and see, Deirdre,' I said. 'Just wait and see.'

'And I must trust you?' she asked.

'If you will. I give you my word that you will be rewarded.'

Big Deirdre folded her meaty arms. 'Then I must be satisfied with that.'

'You have my word.'

'Then you also have mine. I will make sure and certain that your passage through this land is not hindered by those who guard it.'

I ignored Nest's horrified face. I knew what I was doing. Well, I hoped I did, anyway. Now all we had to do was find Gwydion and rescue him. And defeat Conor and Spiderwitch.

Nothing to it.

Keep telling yourself that, *Tanz,* I thought, *maybe you'll end up believing it!*

18

Big Deirdre set off in one direction to talk to the Banshee and all the other scary inhabitants of the Emerald Isle, to get them at least temporarily on our side, and we set off in the other to look for Gwydion, picking up O'Liam along the way. Relief at seeing us arrive safely was written all over his golden little face. Outside the entrance to the Land Beneath, we shifted into ants again. Ants seemed to be able to scurry around without being noticed, and I'm a great believer in 'if it ain't broke, don't fix it!'

We scuttled under the door and into the long earth-floored corridor. We found a place to pause, and Nest and I got our antennae waggling, trying to pick up a trace of Gwydion somewhere in Conor's Kingdom. Neither of us could sense him at all, but somehow I knew he was there. I just had that *feeling*, you know?

So we went looking for him. We thought that the best way of finding him was to go and eavesdrop on Conor and Spiderwitch, wherever they were. We picked up their traces quickly enough: Conor was in one place, Spiderwitch was elsewhere. We thought about splitting up, but decided it was probably safer to stay together. O'Liam was looking nervous in an antsy sort of way, and neither Nest nor I would function too well if we were each worrying about the other!

We found Conor first: he was having his dancing lesson. His long, golden hair was tied back behind his head, and he had a pair of twinkly-buckled shoes on his little feet. A small group of musicians in the corner were playing some jiggety Irish folk music, and Conor was leaping about like a leprechaun possessed. He was doing that bendy thing with his ankles the way Irish dancers do, and trying to keep in time with the leprechaun rattling away on the bodhran drum. Michael Flatley he wasn't, and so he was having a tantrum, blaming the bodhran player for not keeping in time with *him!* Fairly typical of Conor's outlook on life, I suppose. Every now and again he reminded me of a rather small version of Henry VIII – except that he didn't have any wives whose heads he could chop, which was probably just as well!

So then we went to find Spiderwitch. She was a bit harder to find. She'd gone down and down the long winding passageways until she'd found a subterranean cavern big enough to fill with her web. She wasn't in spider-form, though. She also had a chair and a table – and, to my horror, a glass tank full of bumble-bees. She was up to her old tricks again. Pots of thick honey and cream to pour over them before she ate them stood ready on a side table . . . I shuddered, and made a mental note to make sure the bees got away safely.

Spiderwitch, her red-lensed spectacles perched eerily on the end of her bony nose, was busy doing something at the table. Her head was bent over her work, and she was absolutely intent on it.

'What's she up to?' I whispered to Nest.

Nest shrugged. 'Who knows?' she said.

'Whatever she is doing,' O'Liam said fervently, 'it is altogether certain she is up to No Good.'

Well, I wanted to find out anyway. I crawled up the leg of the table and peered over the edge. I didn't put my whole body over, just my antennae and eyes, hoping that she would be too intent on what she was doing to spot a fraction of ant watching her. I couldn't work out what she was at to begin with, and then I suddenly realised. Remember the little wooden box with the hair and nail clippings that we'd found in the Black Castle? Well, that was open in front of her, and she was sticking bits of hair and toenail into a tiny wax model of a person. She was nobbling Conor of the Land Beneath with his own off-cuts! That was real BadWitch style, that was. Once she'd finished, she'd start sticking pins in the model, and wherever she stuck the pin, Conor would feel the pain . . . I almost felt sorry for the Leprechaun Lord. Almost.

I must have let my antennae twitch, because suddenly Spiderwitch's hand shot out and crashed on the table a hair's breadth away from me. Fortunately I was so light that the draught of her hand landing blew me off the table instead of squishing me altogether. I rapidly turned myself into a money-spider and parachuted down on gossamer. Safely on the ground again, I turned back to ant, and reported to the others. We went into a huddle to discuss what our next step should be.

Suddenly, Spiderwitch shoved her chair back and leapt to her feet. Her head was on one side, and she pushed her spectacles back up her nose, the red-tinted glass magnifying her eyes horribly. She sniffed, as if trying to smell something, shut her eyes and sniffed again.

'I smell GoodWitch!' she muttered under her breath. 'She is here. I can smell her. Where is she?'

Well, I hadn't had a shower for a while, but I made

sure I washed as often as I possibly could! Nest tugged my fore-foot and the three of us scuttled frantically for the door. I was suddenly knocked tail-over-antennae by the sweep of Spiderwitch's skirt.

'I can smell her!' she said, her voice rising. The wax image of Conor lay forgotten on her workbench as Spiderwitch flung open the door and marched up the corridor. 'Where is she?' she screamed again.

We followed her, running as fast as we possibly could. Even so, we reached Conor's chamber a fair bit behind her, since ants have only little legs. The two leprechauns guarding the doorway were gazing at the roof and whistling nonchalantly, pretending that they couldn't see her, which was probably very wise of them, since even when she was in a good temper she didn't appreciate being thwarted. Conor, in mid-jig, looked decidedly annoyed at the interruption, but by then Spiderwitch was in full flow.

'She's here, you fool! The GoodWitch is here!'

The musicians straggled to a stop and stood shifting uneasily from foot to foot. Conor brushed an invisible speck of dust off his immaculate white shirt. 'And what if she is? Did you not say that between us we can conquer the world?'

'And so we can. But if the GoodWitch is here, we have her in our power and we shall not need to conquer anything! We can just walk in and take whatever we wish!'

Conor waved a hand to dismiss his nervous musicians, and then looked about with exaggerated interest. 'I can't say that I see her, myself. Do you not think that you may be mistaken, Spiderwitch?'

Merch Corryn Du bent towards the leprechaun king until they were eyeball to eyeball. 'I am *never mistaken*,' she hissed. 'She is here.'

'And would she likely risk coming here knowing that we have the Dragonking as our prisoner?' Conor asked, dabbing his perspiring forehead daintily with a silken hanky.

'Of course she would! She is stupid enough to think she could rescue him,' Spiderwitch said. 'But we shall have her, too. Then, when we have both the Dragonking and his Lady, Ynys Haf is mine!'

'Ours!' Conor reminded her crossly. 'We rule together, Spiderwitch. We made a bargain.'

'So we did, Conor of the Land Beneath,' Spiderwitch whispered, her red-masked eyes glittering. 'So. We. Did.'

Nest and I decided it was time for us to leave. We scuttled out of Conor's chamber, paused under a convenient lump of tree-root and tried to work out what to do next.

My mind was its usual completely blank self. Wherever Gwydion was he seemed to have been shielded from us somehow, but I still couldn't rid myself of the feeling that he was close to us. If only there was someone we could ask. Then I remembered.

O'Liam's Mammy! Maybe she would help us. She'd helped us to find T.A. and Elffin, after all. 'Come on, O'Liam,' I whispered, 'time to visit your dear old Mammy.' We headed down the passage towards Brigid of the Light Fingers' roses-round-the-door room.

We were all out of breath by the time we got there

and scuttled in under the door. Brigid was in her usual chair, rocking and knitting and humming to herself. *Aaah, bless,* I thought, then remembered that the dear little old lady was the Land Beneath's premier pickpocket. I was just about to shift back into myself when Brigid spoke.

'Is it yourself, Lady? And is that Nest with you? How are you, cousin?'

Nest and I streamed upward into our own shapes. 'How did you know we were here?' I asked, as soon as I had vocal chords again.

'I can sense a witch as well as anyone,' Brigid chuckled. 'Are you not going to shift my boy at all?'

I'd completely forgotten O'Liam, being preoccupied with looking for Gwydion. The leprechaun grew up from the ground, green boots first, and gave his Mammy a hug.

'Are you keeping well, now Mammy?' he asked, kissing her cheek. *'Conas tá tú?'*

'Táim go maith, slán go raibh tú,' she replied, putting down her knitting.

'Ah, you're well, good, good,' her son said, plopping down on the footstool beside her and reaching for the biscuit tin. He looked settled for the day.

Brigid put down her knitting and rocked, her arms resting lightly on the chair arms, watching us with bright eyes. 'Would you be here for a purpose?' she asked at last.

'Mammy, did you know the Spiderwitch is here in the Land Beneath, and did you know that she has gone and captured the Dragonking?'

161

'She has, so,' Brigid agreed. 'Should you not be looking for him, then?'

My heart plummeted. Rats. Looked like Brigid didn't know where he was, either. *Then* I remembered that leprechauns are by nature sneaky characters. She wasn't going to volunteer any information, was she?

Flattery sometimes works on little old ladies. 'Well,' I began, 'we've looked for him, and tried to pick him up on our antennae, but we can't find him. I think he's being shielded somehow. But I know he's here somewhere, I'm sure of it. Then I remembered you and I suddenly thought, I'll bet O'Liam's dear, kind Mammy will know something. If only she will help us, I thought.' I tried to look appealing and trustworthy and stuff.

'Ah, hold your old flattery,' Brigid said, picking up her knitting again. 'We have a saying, do we not, O'Liam?'

'We do so, Mammy,' her son replied, nodding sagely. 'We do indeed.'

'And it is?' I said, trying not to grit my teeth.

'There is no need like the lack of a friend,' they replied in chorus.

I closed my eyes briefly. 'But I thought I had a friend in you, O'Liam,' I said piteously, 'and because of our friendship I hoped your Mammy might help us again.'

'You might so, Mammy,' O'Liam said, nodding vigorously. 'It would be a kind thing if you did.'

'I might,' the old lady replied.

We waited.

'I might.'

162

Waited some more.

'I might. I might say, might I not, that you should go from here and turn to your right. Keep going down and down until it is possible to go down no further, and then keep your eyes on the ground. I might say also that, if you should see a trapdoor, you should certainly open it. I might say that you should be altogether wary of doing so, for who can tell what spells might have been laid upon it. I might say that beneath this trapdoor you might possibly see a flight of steps heading downward in an altogether helpful manner. I might say that if you go down these steps, who knows what you might find? I might say all of that.' Brigid knitted hard and fast, the needles clicking.

'But I shall say none of these things, because you are the Lady of a foreign place, and I am a loyal servant to Conor of the Land Beneath. Even if you should do nasty things to me, stick pins in me or threaten me with death I should not say one word.'

'Of course you wouldn't, Brigid of the Light Fingers,' I said, shifting us into ants again. 'But thank you all the same!'

Brigid's voice followed us down the passage. 'Take care, O'Liam, my boy!'

19

So down the corridor we went, until we came to a flight of steps leading down into darkness. I thought it was safe to shift back to ourselves: there was no one about down here, and it would be quicker to negotiate steps with two feet rather than six very small ones. I summoned up a modest moon, and it bobbed ahead of us so that we didn't trip. At the bottom was a door, and behind the door another flight of steps. Down and down we went, the air growing thicker and mustier with every step, and whether it was the exercise or not I don't know, but it seemed to be getting warmer and warmer. But I still couldn't sense Gwydion, not at all.

At the bottom of this flight of steps was a short passageway ending in a blank wall. Obeying Brigid's instructions, we looked down, and sure enough, there was the trapdoor. I decided the safest way to open it was probably with magic, so I got the others to stand well back against the walls, while I zapped the wooden trap-door with a spell which silently blew it clean off. Just as Brigid had said, a flight of steps led down and down. 'Come on,' I said, took a deep breath, and put my foot down into the hole.

'Ow!' I said, jumping back. My foot vibrated and throbbed like a funny-bone.

'What happened?' Nest asked, alarmed.

'Felt like an electric shock!' I moaned, rubbing my tortured toes. 'Spiderwitch has probably put a spell on the stairs themselves. I'd assumed it would be in the trapdoor, for some reason.'

'We have a saying,' O'Liam began.

'Thought you might,' I said, my teeth thoroughly gritted, half with pain, half with the prospect of another O'Liam saying.

'Never assume. Assuming will make an "ass" out of both "u" and "me",' he said solemnly, his finger raised.

'Thanks a bunch, O'Liam. Now, how are we going to get down that hole? If it's a spell, then we should be able to break it. Unless of course the Spiderwitch has discovered electricity.'

'And what would that be when it's at home?' O'Liam enquired.

'Tell you some other time, O'Liam. Nest, have you got any ideas?' I tried putting weight on my injured foot. It felt a bit dead, as if it had gone to sleep, but it seemed O.K. otherwise.

Nest walked round the hole, thinking. 'If Gwydion is down there, then it's a two-way spell: it will stop him getting out, at the same time as stopping us getting in. So I think we'd better tackle it in two parts. Since she didn't expect us to be here, it's probably just a simple force field sort of spell. If we can get rid of that and get down, we should be able to fix the getting-out spell when we want to leave.'

Nest was right, at least about the first part. I closed my eyes and thought up the spell to clear force fields. It would have been quicker if I'd had a jar of clover honey and some Common Earthstar fungus, but it worked as well with just will-power, luckily. When I was pretty sure that the force field had gone, I cautiously poked a toe over the edge, wincing in anticipation, just in case. Nothing.

'It's O.K. It worked. We can go down now.'

I sent the moon down first, and started down the steps. A strange, musty, heavy smell rose up, vaguely familiar, not pleasant, and it made me feel a bit on edge. The walls on either side of us were made of earth packed so hard that they seemed to shine as if they'd been polished, and the tunnel was completely round as if it had been done with a giant Black and Decker drill. Half way down the wooden steps I began to pick up a faint trace of Gwydion's presence. 'He's here!' I said, joyfully.

Down and down we went, our feet echoing on the stairs, and the sense of Gwydion being close – and, unfortunately, the unpleasant smell – grew stronger and stronger. I know it was probably dumb, but I couldn't help calling out his name.

And he answered! Unfortunately, however, it wasn't an answer that particularly cheered me up.

'Tanz? Is that you?'

'Me and Nest and O'Liam!' I bellowed back.

'Stop where you are! Don't come any closer!' he yelled, and I heard a note of panic in his voice.

'What? Don't you want to be rescued?' I said stupidly.

'Of course I do, you idiot. But it's too dangerous.'

'Dangerous? Why?'

'I can't say why. It's asleep at the moment, but it recognises its name and that will wake it. But look around you, Tanz. At the walls and the ceiling and floor.'

What on earth was he on about? I looked round me. Nothing but a perfectly round passageway, so round that it might have been made by a giant earthwoooooooooorm! My feet started telling me to run. I ignored them. I could tell by Nest's face that she'd cottoned on, too, and O'Liam was making a strategic withdrawal up the steps. All at once I identified the smell: the reptile house at the zoo . . .

'Gwydion,' I said, my voice for some reason having acquired a bit of a tremor, 'are you trying to tell me that you have something s-s-s-scary there with you?'

'You could say that,' he said, faintly.

'Is it very long? And about as round as the tunnel? And does it have scales?'

'And teeth,' he said, nervously.

'Will it understand if I spell out what I think it is?'

'Probably not,' he said patiently, 'I don't think it can read.'

'Is it the G-R-E-A-T W-O-R-M O-F M-U-L-L-I-N-G-A-R, Gwydion?'

'More like its big brother, Tanz.'

'O-H S-H-O-O-T,' I moaned.

'You can stop spelling now, Tanz. You've got the general idea.'

Horrified, I looked at Nest and O'Liam. 'I thought Big Deirdre was going to fix all the local wildlife!' I said indignantly.

'Well, maybe she missed this one.'

'This will not be the Great Worm of Mullingar,' O'Liam said shakily. 'No, not a Mullingar at all. It will be the Great Worm of Conor's Great, great, great-Grandaddy. Didn't he keep it as a pet?'

'I know, don't tell me. It got too big for the house and he turned it loose,' I said.

'Isn't that the way of inconvenient pets like dragons? No consideration at all.'

'D-dragons?' I said.

'Well, what else is a Great Worm if it isn't a dragon?'

'Fiery breath and all that?'

'Exactly. I remember seeing it once my very own self, and an alarming sight altogether it was, so.'

I took a deep breath. 'Right. Right. Right.' Inside, I was thinking, *ohhelpohhelpohhelp,* but nothing actually did, unfortunately. 'Don't worry, Gwyd,' I bellowed. 'I'll think of something!'

'Good,' Gwydion's voice echoed faintly back. 'I'm a bit keen to get out of here. Before it gets hungry again . . .'

I went hot and cold and hot. I stared helplessly at Nest and O'Liam, and they stared just as helplessly back.

'What do we do?' I asked. 'What do big, nasty male dragons *like?*'

'Food, sleep and other dragons of the female persuasion, in that order,' O'Liam said. 'And we could be the first, can't do the second, and aren't the third.'

'But we could be!' I said, suddenly having an idea.

'What, food?' O'Liam said, anxiously, 'I don't think I'm in favour of that idea at all, Lady, if you don't mind.'

'Not *food*, O'Liam. A lady dragon!'

'It would be horribly risky, Tanith,' Nest said. 'I don't think it's a good idea.'

'It's a terrible idea,' I agreed. 'But can you think of anything else?'

Nest thought hard, then slowly shook her head. 'Unfortunately, no.'

'Right then. Let's see if I can work out how to shift into dragonshape . . .'

It took a long, long time. It made my head ache. I got the shape all right, but couldn't manage the scales at the same time. Then I got the scales and the shape went wrong. At last, I finally managed to put the two together. I was about twenty metres of lady dragon, with pink and silver iridescent scales – that seemed suitably girly, even for a dragon – and a beautiful set of gleaming white choppers. I had three horns on my forehead, and I had to be very careful when I breathed out. I coughed, and nearly set fire to O'Liam's boots, but he finally agreed that I was the very image of Conor's Great Worm – as far as he remembered – only female.

O'Liam was trying to hide behind Nest. Even knowing the dragon was me, he still wasn't too keen.

I took a deep breath and winked at Nest. 'Here I go!' I said, tried to paste an amorous lady dragon expression on my face, and slithered into the tunnel, followed at a distance by the other two. I didn't have feet, I wasn't that sort of a dragon. I was sort of long and worm-shaped, with coils like a boa-constrictor. My scales rustled against the tunnel walls as I went, and I realised how they had become so smooth and polished . . .

The tunnel went on for a way, and then widened out into a cave, its walls sparkling with mineral deposits, and a second tunnel leading off the opposite side. In the centre of the tunnel was a great heap of shimmering coils. The dragon's head was tucked beneath one of them, and right next to him, chained to the wall – with iron chains of course, since white magic could do nothing with iron, was Gwydion. He was unshaven, dirty, and I don't think he'd had much to eat for a while. His eyes widened in horror when he saw me – not knowing it was me, of course. He probably thought he was going to be a running buffet – or a chained-up one for two dragons. I sent a thought-wave over and he grinned with relief.

I'm going to get you out of here!

Good! How? he thought back.

Sex appeal!

But you haven't . . .

Shut up, Gwyd!

The Great Worm snored and shifted a coil. If I wanted to lead him away from Gwydion so that O'Liam (who had no problems with iron, of course) could release him to run for it, I had to wake him up. I took a deep breath and slithered over to the sleeping monster.

'Ah-hem!' I said, then, too late, remembered my fiery breath. A jet of flame just missed Gwydion, and he yelped. The dragon stirred again, but didn't wake. There was nothing else for it. I slithered closer and gave him a mighty shove.

A couple of coils slithered off the heap, and one of them, in passing, clouted the sleeping Great Worm around the ear. He coughed, twitched, and his eyes fluttered open. They were alarming eyes. They were huge, the size of dustbin lids, with black where the whites should have been. The irises were golden with black, elongated pupils, and they were very, very scary. They locked onto mine, which I knew were exactly the same – O'Liam had told me what eyes to have. Looking into them, rather than out of them was mega scary, right?

Like I said, the Great Worm's eyes locked onto mine. I fluttered my eyelashes and wiggled my coils. The Great Worm blinked, and a dopy smile spread across its face. It straightened up, its eyes still gazing into mine. Looked like I'd made a conquest! Some enchanted evening, across a crowded room and all that.

The dragon uncoiled its scales and undulated as if it were dancing. It writhed and twisted, all the time its eyes on mine. I was so fascinated at the graceful movements it was making that I didn't realise it was getting closer and closer . . .

Then suddenly I did. *Oops!* I thought, gathered my coils and headed for the exit. Time to play hard to get!

20

The tunnel in the other direction was just as long, but instead of stairs there was a steep incline upward – to the surface, I hoped. The trouble was that while I could coil perfectly well, and bat my eyelashes and stuff, as soon as it came to running – or slithering – for my life, I wasn't very good at that. I couldn't get the hang of co-ordinating my coils. I kept getting a loop stuck, or my scales would overlap and lock so that I couldn't straighten out. The result was that the Great Worm was gaining on me. I stretched my neck out and tried to go faster.

Then I felt a set of teeth close – gently – on my tail. 'Aaaaargh!' I screamed, but of course, being a dragon, it didn't come out like that. Instead, a blast of searing flame scorched the walls ahead of me. The teeth weren't *biting*, exactly. More just holding on in a playful manner the way a person play-wrestling might hold gently on to another person's ankle if he tried to crawl away. And the Great Worm, perhaps thinking I was playing hard to get, was gently but determinedly pulling me back into his lair . . .

I flung myself forward and tried to haul myself loose. It let go, and for a second I thought I was free, but then I felt it take hold again a bit higher up my tail. It was overtaking me! The trouble was, the tunnel was such a tight fit that I couldn't turn round and frizzle it. I could only go forward, and that was becoming increasingly difficult.

'Nest!' I bellowed, 'heeeeeelp!' Unfortunately, Nest

couldn't hear me, or didn't understand dragon-talk, because nothing happened. I inched desperately towards the light at the end of the tunnel, and at last managed to struggle my front end into the open air. A large oak tree grew a few metres away, and I made a final effort to wrap myself around it, use it as an anchor, and drag my tail free. Just as the Great Worm shot out of the tunnel after me, I collected my wits, shimmered, and shifted into a sparrow. I shot up the oak, sat on a branch and leaned against the trunk, panting in panic. The Great Worm stopped short as I disappeared, an expression of acute mystification on its face. It twined around the base of the tree, shaking loose a load of acorns, and poked its head into a bush or two. Then it disconsolately turned its coils around and headed back down the tunnel.

Towards Nest, O'Liam and Gwydion. Oh, no! O'Liam would certainly need more time than he'd had, to convince the iron shackles tethering Gwydion to the cave wall to let him go. I flung myself out of the branches, and shifted back into Great Worm Lady. It was easier this time – I had the feel of it. I shot back into the tunnel and grabbed the end of a disappearing tail. Unfortunately I wasn't quite as good at controlling my bite as the Great Worm – I sank my pearly-whites deep – through tough scales and into the flesh beneath. The dragon gave an anguished roar, and its body writhed in pain. It couldn't turn, fortunately, so it shot forward instead, dragging me with it. In the cave I heard a terrified scream, recognised O'Liam's voice, and just managed to wrap the very last coil of my tail round the oak tree and hold on. It stopped the Great Worm with a jerk, like a dog on the end of a lead. I sent thought-waves along the tunnel to Nest, *Get Gwydion loose and get out of there! I don't know how much longer I can hold on!*

She sent back *O'Liam's a gibbering wreck. He just got his bottom singed when the dragon roared. But he's carrying on. Just hang on, Tanz. For goodness sake, hang on!'*

Too right I was going to hang on. If I let go, the Great Worm would either go forward or back, and either would be disastrous! I hauled experimentally, managed to get a better grip on the tree, and hauled again. Centimetre by centimetre I began to drag the Great Worm backward out of the tunnel. I didn't, of course, want him all the way out. Just far enough out so that he couldn't barbecue O'Liam, Gwydion and Nest.

How are you getting on? I thought-waved, grimly hanging on.

Nearly there! came back at me.

Inside the cave I heard the rattle of chains falling loose, and the sound of running feet.

Just hang on a bit longer, Tanz, Nest sent, *until we can get up the stairs. As soon as we're out, I'll let you know.*

I dug my teeth in harder, and the dragon writhed. My jaw was aching with the strain of keeping it clamped shut. It seemed ages before a faraway voice whispered in my head, *We're out, Tanz! You can let go now!*

I took a deep breath through my nose, and let go. The tail disappeared up the tunnel like a rat up a drainpipe, the dragon turned, and seconds later a furious head shot out, roaring flame ahead of it. By that time I'd changed into a sparrow, and shot over its head and down the tunnel, through the now empty cave and up the wooden stairs. The trouble was that the trapdoor at the top of the stairs had been firmly shut.

Thanks a bunch, guys! I thought. They must have expected me to go round the long way, back in through the main entrance to the Land Beneath, and not shoot back the way I'd come. I couldn't zap the trapdoor in bird-shape, I'd have to shift to myself and zap it. I could hear the sound of the Great Worm roaring along behind me, and the air was getting distinctly hot as he set fire to the wooden stairs. Smoke drifted upwards, and I coughed as I shifted into myself. Through streaming eyes I squinted at the trapdoor and gabbled a spell to open it. Nothing happened. Flames licked around the bottom bit of the flight of stairs I was standing on. I thumped it with my fist, hearing the dragon coming nearer. 'Open, you stupid damn thing!' I shrieked, and bellowed the spell again. This time, it shot open, and I was through it like greased lightning. I slammed it shut and sealed it with a spell. Smoke drifted round the edges of the wood, but I was safe.

I pelted up the long corridor behind the others, and came up with them just as they drew level with O'Liam's Mammy's door. Little clouds and puffs of smoke infiltrated the corridor behind us. We knocked on the door and burst in. Brigid was still knitting and rocking.

'Ah, you found your man, so,' she said calmly. 'That's good, is it not? Would that be smoke I can smell, now?'

'The Great Worm set fire to the stairway,' I said, panting and wiping my eyes.

'Ah, did it so?' Brigid put down her knitting. 'Would it be a good idea to evacuate the premises at all, do you know?'

I looked at Gwydion and Nest. 'Would it?' I stammered.

'Might be a good idea to get out of here,' Gwydion said. 'If we all get roasted, we can't do a lot to save Ynys Haf, right?'

'Come on, Mammy!' O'Liam grabbed his mother's arm and tried to hustle her to the door.

'Surely you don't think I'll go empty-handed as the way I came into this world?' Brigid enquired indignantly. 'There are a few wee things I will take if you don't mind.'

Which is why, several long, smoky, choky minutes later, Gwydion, O'Liam, Nest and I staggered out of Brigid's home piled high with miscellaneous bundles: clothing, pots and pans, jewellery, the rocking chair, a large number of useful plastic items including buckets, bowls, Tupperware containers and credit cards, none of which would be invented for about a thousand years. Goodness knows how Brigid had come by those. The passageway was full of thick, black smoke.

'Gwydion,' I said, alarmed, 'what if the whole Land Beneath catches fire?'

'Serves Conor right for keeping a dragon in the basement,' he said coolly.

'But what about the people that aren't like him? People like O'Liam, and those nice little serving girls, and the cook and the maids and the tweenies in the kitchen?' I protested. 'And the musicians and his secrechauns?'

'Oh, rats!' Gwydion moaned. 'I suppose we've got to warn them, have we?'

'Well, of course we have!' Nest frowned. 'We can't leave them to suffocate or burn, can we?'

So I magicked up a huge fire-bell and a big stick, and I beat it and beat it and shouted 'Fire, fire!' until the passageways reverberated with sound and little people came running from all directions, panicking madly, intent on saving themselves.

And so did Spiderwitch and Conor. They stopped short when they saw us, and Spiderwitch's eyes narrowed.

'So, Dragonking, you escaped!' she hissed.

'Of course,' Gwydion said loftily. 'I'm the Good Guy. Good Guys always escape.'

Not that you had any help, Gwydion, I thought. Ungrateful pig!

'Then escape this, Dragonking!' she snarled, and threw a spell at us. In the confines of the tunnel we were almost helpless, and instinctively ducked in case the spell hit us. But it didn't reach us. Instead, it dropped harmlessly to the ground. Spiderwitch didn't wait to see it land. She was already legging it up the tunnel away from the flames, closely followed by Conor and a long stream of panicky leprechauns.

'Ha! Missed us!' I crowed, and took a step forward. Instantly a vast iron door shot from the ground in front of me, floor to ceiling, sealing us in with the deadly smoke and flames. And then, horror of horrors, out of the ground between us and the door came hundreds of large, sinister, spidery shapes.

Tarantulas!

Naturally I screamed very loudly, and tried to climb up Gwydion, since I'm not at all fond even of quite small arachnids. And these were not small. They were extraordinarily large, and hairy, and red-eyed, and befanged, and they kept coming, so I screamed again, only louder.

'Shut up, Tanz,' Gwydion said, disentangling himself from me. 'Screaming won't help.'

'I know that,' I said, trying not to squinch my eyes shut and disappear into a quivering, panicky blob. 'But it makes me feel better!'

By now the iron in the door was beginning to get to me, too. I started to feel sick and shaky. This was it. The end of the whole Adventure. Goodbye world. Goodbye, Gwydion, Nest, O'Liam and the Mammy. Goodbye me!

Gwydion shoved me behind him and stamped very hard on a large tarantula. As soon as he took his boot off it, however, it stood up and walked away. 'Oh,' he said, taken aback. 'Nest, can you get rid of the wildlife?'

When I heard that, I opened one eye. Gave myself a severe talking to. They were only magical spiders, right? What had been conjured up could be got rid of. I thought of Groovy Bill Shakespeare, summoned up my blood and stiffened up my sinews. I stood shoulder to shoulder with Nest and between us we vanished several hundred large, hairy spiders. We only just managed it, because the iron door was beginning to affect both of us, and our magic was weakening by the second. When the last one was gone, we were choking on thick clouds of acrid smoke, coughing, eyes streaming, and the effect of the iron door getting worse and worse.

'O'Liam,' I spluttered, 'it's up to you, now. Can you fix that iron?'

'Oh, I can so,' he said, put down Brigid's rocking chair and rolled up his sleeves. His Mammy sat down, got out her knitting and did a few rows.

'How can you knit at a time like this?' I howled.

'Oh, 'tis easy, Lady!' she chortled. 'You put the wee needle in like so, put the woolly bit over, wrap it round the two needles like so, pull the loop through and chase the other one off the one below.'

O'Liam marched up to the door, and placed his small golden hand flat against it. 'Ah, I know this iron!' he said, brightening. 'It's a good style of metal altogether, but it needs a telling-off for getting involved with a bad influence. Iron,' he said sternly, 'do you know who your Master is?'

The iron groaned like a bull elephant.

'Well, so? What are you doing hanging about here and confounding us all?'

The iron groaned again.

'What like are you, iron? Are you a metal or a mouse? Do you hear who is talking to you?'

With a final groan the great door slid down into the floor. I felt better instantly. The way was clear, the passageway empty – except for the choking torrents of black smoke.

'Right,' I said happily. 'Let's get out of here!'

They didn't need to be told twice. We all legged it like Jamie Baulch on top form.

21

We weren't daft, though. We didn't go romping merrily out into the open air in our own shapes. We shoved all Brigid's possessions up close to the doorway, then shifted everyone except Brigid into mice and shot out underneath the pile of assorted stuff. Brigid hollered orders at the top of her voice and a dozen leprechauns bravely wrestled her rocking chair and all the other junk out of the doorway and released her from the smoky passageway. No one thought to ask how a little old lady had managed to haul all that junk out of the lower reaches of the Land Beneath. Maybe they thought, hey, well, this is Brigid of the Light Fingers we're talking about. She can do anything!

But then things got a bit hairy. Once she was out, and Conor set eyes upon her, he obviously remembered that the last time he'd seen her, she'd been with us – and on the other side of the iron door. And if Brigid was here, then equally obviously, even for his pea-brain, so were we . . .

He bellowed an order, and two hefty guards went to grab the harmless little old lady. Did I say harmless? Well, I suppose if you're the finest pickpocket in the kingdom, one of the first things you learn during your apprenticeship is probably how to scarper, fast. As they stretched out their arms to grab her she bent down and scuttled underneath. Then she spun, quite athletically for a dear-little-old-lady, on her heel and kicked one in a particularly painful place, and did the neatest karate chop on the other that I've ever seen. Leaving one groaning and the other unconscious, she legged it in the general direction of away.

Conor immediately set half a dozen more guards onto her. When they started gaining on her I thought it might be a good plan to shift her, fast, into a mouse. Brigid, quick on the uptake, shot down a hole and the guards were left looking befuddled.

Conor screamed with fury and threw a tantrum, hurling himself about, shrieking and stamping his feet (not both at once: he'd have fallen over). If I'd ever behaved like that, Mam would have walloped my backside and sent me to bed. Spiderwitch folded her arms, watched him for a few seconds, and then – winked out of the Land Beneath like a switched-off light.

'She's gone, Gwydion!' I squeaked. 'Where did she go?'

'Didn't see,' he squeaked back, his whiskers whiffling. 'But I didn't think she'd hang around here long. Did you see what she was carrying?'

I hadn't. 'What?'

'The only thing she brought out from Conor's kingdom was the little silver box with his nails and hair in it. And probably the wax doll, too. So she still has him in her power. I think she's probably on her way to Ynys Haf right now.'

'Then what are we hanging about here for?'

'Are we going to let the Land Beneath burn?'

'No. It's too many people's homes, as well as Conor's. But we'll leave the smoke as a distraction. Conor will be too busy worrying about that for a while to bother about invading Ynys Haf. Everyone is safely outside so no one's going to die from smoke inhalation. So we can maybe tackle Spiderwitch while she's on her own.'

I concentrated hard on a cold water spell in the dragon's cave, and when my senses told me the fire was out, magicked up clouds of thick, clogging smoke so that the leprechaun firefighters wouldn't discover too quickly that there wasn't any fire to put out. Then we headed for the coast, and didn't stop off at Big Deirdre's on the way. I'd come back soon enough if everything went well in Ynys Haf. Then I could give her the reward I planned – providing she kept the local Banshees and suchlike away from us. I had a feeling that Conor might enlist anything and everything that lurked in his underworld to defeat us if he had to.

When we reached the coast, we saw that the sea was rough, waves hurling themselves enthusiastically onto the rocks and shattering in great plumes of spray. O'Liam (and I) turned green at the sight of it. His Mammy certainly wouldn't be able to swim or fly the distance across the Middlesome Sea, and so there was only one thing for it: Nest, O'Liam, Gwydion and I shifted into shearwaters, shifted Brigid into a mouse, and Gwydion picked her up in his beak. We skimmed low over the stormy seas, our white undersides matching the white horses galloping in the heaving waves beneath us.

We hurtled towards Ynys Haf, and every wingbeat of the way, the weather grew worse. Soon the wind was howling in our faces, the waves having turned from choppy white horses to great rolling swells, and the rain lashed down. Approaching Cantre'r Gwaelod, a feeling of dread crept over me. I began to get a sick feeling in my stomach. Merlin had changed the weather with a vengeance: Ynys Haf's dry spell was over, but he seemed to have overdone it. The surging rivers would be threatening Cantre'r Gwaelod as well as the rushing, swelling, incoming tide.

And then I saw that the great sluice gates protecting the Sixteen Cities of Cantre'r Gwaelod were open to the storm, and wild, rushing floodwaters were already gushing through the streets.

And T.A., Taliesin, Elffin, Gwyddno, Lady Gwyddno and all the people were there. Oh, and Maebh, of course.

With a scream of alarm I plunged onward towards Gwyddno's tower. The water was already two or three metres up the wall, and the wall itself was crumbling as the weight of the torrential water pounded at it. Followed by the others, I swooped in through an upper window, shifted into myself and began screaming for T.A. at the top of my voice. There was no answer. I ran frantically from room to room, but there was no sign of anyone. A legend was being born – with a sick feeling, I remembered what had happened.

Gwyddno had held a huge party, probably to celebrate the end of the drought. If only I'd disobeyed Taliesin and Merlin and warned him! Would he have believed me? Everyone in the Sixteen Cities except the gatekeeper had been invited to the celebration. The waters had broken through, and everyone had drowned, except Taliesin, who turned into a white owl and escaped from his tower. Did that mean that T.A.

was already dead? She was from another Time, she had no part in the legend – but had she been trapped nonetheless? I went cold at the thought.

Taliesin's tower! If that was where he was, then maybe he hadn't escaped yet. Maybe he'd know where she was. I hurtled out through another window – the waters were still rising and the window I'd come in by was already under water.

Only the tops of the towers were still visible. Taliesin's was the tallest of all. I didn't even look to see if Nest and Gwydion were following: they could take care of themselves. T.A. is my friend, and I was going to get her out of this. She shouldn't be here. She shouldn't die. My heart was breaking for our friend Gwyddno and for Elffin, but T.A. was my main concern. I had to save T.A.

I hurled myself through the storm, my wings barely able to force me forward through the hammering wind and rain. Lightning flashed all round me, and dimly through the torrential downpour I saw Gwydion and Nest hovering over the sluice gates, perhaps trying desperately to think of some way to get them closed against the terrible tide. But nature is as strong a force as magic, and exerts its own power: control of the weather and its effects was the hardest spell for any witch or warlock – even Merlin, the greatest of them all. And he seemed to have overdone it.

At last I struggled to the window of the tall alabaster tower, and flopped through it, exhausted. I shifted into myself, my heart pounding with relief.

T.A. and Maebh were huddled in the corner, clinging to each other. Well, Maebh was clinging to

T.A., anyway. T.A. was busy being T.A., brave to the last. Well, it wasn't going to be the last, not if I had anything to do with it.

T.A. spotted me and screamed with mingled shock and joy.

'Tanz! What are you doing here? Oh, thank goodness!'

'Where's Taliesin? He's supposed to be here!'

'He is!' she shouted back, over the howl of the wind and the beat of the rain. 'He's outside on the stairs. We tried to drag him up with us, but he was too heavy and the stairs are too awkward. We got him up as high as we could.'

'Drag him?' I yelled back, 'Why? Is he hurt?'

'He was trying to guide us to safety,' she screamed, 'and a tower collapsed and a stone hit him on the head. I think he's alive, but I couldn't wake him up!'

So this was the reason for T.A.'s presence in this Time: Mam and the Ant had said she was here for a purpose, and saving Taliesin had to be it. I ran for the doorway and peered down the stairs. Only Taliesin's head, the hair above his ear matted with seeping blood, was visible because of the curve of the stairs. I went down to him, and saw that the rising water had already covered his legs to above his knees.

I stooped, rested my fingers against his throat, feeling the reassuring throb of his pulse beating. Alive, then, but deeply unconscious and helpless to save himself.

'He's alive!' I screamed over my shoulders. I swiftly shifted him into a mouse and carried the bedraggled, bleeding little creature cupped in my hands back up to the tower where T.A. and Maebh waited. The wind shoved rudely in through the windows and the force was enough to stir the vast silver bell dangling from the roof-beams. The sound of the tongue striking the metal echoed mournfully over the rising flood.

There was no time to talk. I shifted us all into white owls – what else? A legend is a legend, and so we had to live up to it – and the three of us, me with Taliesin held gently in my beak, flew silently out into the storm just as the torrent of water gushed into the tower room.

Gwydion and Nest had abandoned their attempts to close the sluice gate: the natural force of the sea was too strong even for their magic. Collecting O'Liam, who was holding his Mammy gently in his beak while perched on a rapidly disappearing chunk of masonry, we left the drowning city and fled to high ground, where we found shelter in a cave. Exhausted, we shifted back.

Maebh lay down, rolled onto her back and fell asleep, her hand across her eyes. Gwydion and T.A., however, were white-faced and grim, and O'Liam and his Mammy sat side by side, unusually subdued, while Nest and I worked on Taliesin to bring him round. His long body was limp and seemingly lifeless: we staunched the head-wound's bleeding and Nest tenderly felt his skull, probing gently for dents that shouldn't be there. She bathed his head, muttered spells, administered herbs from the pouch at her belt. At last, he stirred and sat up dizzily, clutching his head.

'What happened?' he groaned. 'The last thing I

remember is trying to get Maebh out of a doorway. She was hanging on like grim death, screaming, and I was trying to peel her fingers from the frame.'

'She was afraid she'd drown if she left the palace,' T.A. said grimly. 'I told her that she was more likely to drown if she stayed, because I'd read the legend, but it didn't make any difference. She was beyond listening by that stage. She is such a total *wimp*, that girl.'

Gwydion magicked a fire and I provided great bowls of steaming soup and fresh bread rolls. It was what we all needed: we couldn't talk, we were too flattened by grief at the loss of our dear friends for that. Although none of us – even Maebh, who was still whimpering softly to herself when she woke at the smell of food – felt as if we'd ever eat again, the rich smell of the hot soup tempted us, and we all felt better for it. As my Mam always says, 'Get it down you, it will do you good'. And it did.

Afterwards, I held T.A.'s hand and squeezed. 'I'm *so, so, sorry* about Elffin, T.A.,' I whispered comfortingly. 'I know how fond you were of him –'

'What, Elffin? Don't talk to me about *him*!' she retorted.

'But he's –'

'Dead? Oh no he isn't. He's gone off on some wild goose chase because of some female!'

I stared at her, blankly. 'He's what? What are you talking about? Elffin drowned with the rest of his family and the people of Cantre'r Gwaelod. It said so, in the legend.'

'Did it? Did it say, specifically, Elffin, son of Gwyddno Garanhir, drowned? Bet it didn't. Anyway, it also said in the legend that Taliesin changed into a white owl and flew out of his tower, and of all the people in Cantre'r Gwaelod, only he escaped, right?'

I nodded.

'Well, that bit was wrong, wasn't it? We flew him out, didn't we? And Elffin isn't dead. At least, not as far as I know, anyway, unless he's fallen off his horse and broken his stupid neck. We were walking on the sea wall – you know, holding hands and stuff, the way you do – and he suddenly spotted this female, trying to drown herself.'

'Sorry, you've lost me.'

'Yes, well. You aren't the only one, Tanz. He dived in and rescued her and hey, nonny nonny and all that, Elffin's in love, and not with me. Love at first sight and all that junk. Can't live without her sort of thing. Goodbye T.A., nice knowing you. He had her carried to his chamber and he slept outside her door all night. But in the morning she'd somehow managed to leg it. Or disappeared, or something, since Elffin's room is right at the top of the tower and the only way out was over his body and she certainly didn't wake him when she went. So Elffin went pootling off, all lovesick, to find Merlin and ask his advice, and he hasn't come back yet.'

'Oh, poor Elffin,' I murmured.

'Humph! Oh, I feel so sorry for him. It's awful, tragic, that all his family is probably dead – but I still want to smack him. I've been dumped, Tanz! Me! Dumped! For some cat-faced little shrimp that tried to drown herself! Honestly, men are such idiots.'

There were times when I felt my best friend had difficulties with her sense of proportion . . .

22

Once we were rested, Gwydion, Nest, Taliesin and I shifted into black-backed gulls and soared out over Cantre'r Gwaelod, needing somehow to see if we could do anything, even though we knew it was unlikely. Grief lay like a heavy weight in my chest. We left the others huddled in the cave.

The sky above us was massed with angry black clouds as we circled slowly over swirling sea water where once there had been green, lush fields daisy-dotted with sheep; deer parks, orchards, silver ribbons of river winding to the sea. Now there was nothing left of any of it, just a vast expanse of turbulent, still-rising water. The bodies of drowned cattle turned lazily in the swell, but the people of Cantre'r Gwaelod must have been trapped in their towers. They would probably never be recovered and buried. Perhaps that was fitting: they had lived with the sea all their lives, it was right that it should be their resting place.

I flew low over the surface, remembering my friends, the people I had come to know, the sunlit hall that had always been filled with laughter, and Gwyddno Garanhir's loyalty to Gwydion, his High King.

The water was clouded by sand swirling up from the bottom, raised by the angry sea, but I could just see, a few metres below the surface, the white marble summit of Taliesin's tower, ghostly and distorted by the refraction of the water. There was nothing we could do; no one we could save. We were not needed here.

We saw no sign of Elffin: I hoped that he had survived, even if his new girlfriend hadn't. There should be someone to carry the Garanhir name into the future.

When we arrived back at the cave, O'Liam and his Mammy sat huddled together, the leprechaun's arm round the tiny woman's frail shoulders. And then I realised that someone was missing.

'Where's Maebh?' I demanded.

O'Liam looked guilty. 'Well, now, and how should I know a thing like that?' he demanded defensively. 'Wasn't I asleep entirely, and when I woke up she had made herself as scarce as snow in summer. We have a saying for it, do we not, Mammy?'

'I'm sure you do, O'Liam,' I said, forestalling another quotation. 'The little rat-bag! Done a runner, has she? Well, that does it. That's the very last time I trust her to behave herself. After all we've done for her, too. Well, we'd better head back to Castell Du straight away. Goodness knows what sort of mischief she'll be getting up to, running around loose.'

Despite the clouds, the weather was slowly improving. The relentless rain had stopped, and the blustering winds were beginning to abate. 'If we take plenty of rest stops, Brigid of the Light Fingers, do you think you could manage to fly?' I asked.

The old lady put her white head on one side. 'Well, now. I will not know unless I try, will I? And as the saying is, "A skill not learned is an enemy".'

I should have known one of them would manage to slip one in.

'That's the spirit!' I said, more heartily than I felt,

and shifted O'Liam and his Mammy into rooks, then, along with Gwydion and Nest, shifted myself. We hopped outside the cave and took off into a watery sun just beginning to break through the clouds. The loss of Cantre'r Gwaelod was a dull ache in my middle: I had tried so hard to save it, for the awful legend not to come true, but it seemed that although minor things could be altered, nothing that I or anyone else did could have prevented the terrible disaster. Nest was silent and withdrawn: Lady Garanhir had been her cousin, and I knew she would grieve for her, and for her kind husband.

However, as we flew over Ynys Haf, I could see that although Merlin had sort of got carried away with the weather spell, the effects were not all as disastrous as what had happened to the Sixteen Cities of Cantre'r Gwaelod. The rivers were lapping at their banks once more, and already a tender greenness was creeping over the land where, only a few days ago, it had been yellow and parched.

By the time we landed in the courtyard of Castell Du we were all exhausted, and glad to shimmer and shift. Flissy came out to greet us, smiling a welcome, and I realised with a sinking feeling that she didn't know what had happened to Cantre'r Gwaelod. I took both her hands in mine and tried to smile back, hating to bring her bad news. 'Fliss, dear Fliss, I'm afraid there's bad news –'

'If you mean that Cantre'r Gwaelod has been drowned,' a voice said, 'then it's just the fulfilling of a legend. You knew it would happen. Why so sentimental?'

I quite often wanted to smack Merlin for one reason or another, but right now I wanted to strangle him, then shoot him, and then possibly jump up and down on his body. Then, possibly, do the whole thing again.

Flissy gasped with shock, and her hands flew up to cover her mouth. 'Oh, Tansy, no! Are they all gone?'

'Everyone except Elffin, apparently,' I said. 'Elffin had a problem he thought Merlin could help him with. I imagine you broke the news just as sympathetically to him, right, Merlin? Sort of, "Oh, by the way, your whole family is dead, tough luck"?'

Merlin frowned. 'Sarcasm does not become you, Tanith. Besides, I haven't seen Elffin.'

It was T.A.'s turn to look worried. 'What do you mean, you haven't seen him? He was heading here!'

'Well, since I haven't seen him, he obviously didn't arrive. Now, if you'll excuse me, I need to go out into Ynys Haf and heal anything else that needs healing. I can't stand around gossiping all day. Oh, and Tanith,' he said, pausing in the doorway of his tower, 'you still have to sort out Spiderwitch. That's entirely up to you – oh, and Gwydion, of course.'

Gwydion's teeth were clenched, and so were his fists. If Merlin hadn't made himself scarce, I think there might have been quite a confrontation, because Gwydion was seriously angry. His face was white, except for two little pink spots high up on his cheekbones.

'Calm down, Gwyd,' I said, patting him sympathetically. 'You know he considers himself an element, like earth, air, fire and water. He can't be expected to have human feelings.'

'All the same,' the Dragonking said softly, 'sooner or later I think Merlin is going to get his come-uppance. I'm not sure how, but –'

'Oh, I know already what happens to Merlin,' I said smugly. 'And trust me, Gwyd, he gets what's coming to him. It's like, serious porridge.'

'Porridge?' Gwydion, Nest, O'Liam and Mammy said simultaneously. 'Porridge?'

Only T.A., Flissy and Taliesin smiled conspiratorially at me. Having come from the future themselves, they, too, knew exactly what happened to Merlin! The funny thing was, that since Merlin himself was able to pop in and out of the Time Doors, then he must know, too. And he was powerless to do anything about it. Actually, in a way, that made it better. See how *he* liked a legend happening to *him*!

What I wanted more than anything was a nice, hot shower. Since they hadn't been invented yet, and I didn't have the energy to magic one up, I made do with a deep tub and a lot of hot water. Clean at last, with my hair washed and French-plaited back (it would take hours to dry, but so what?) I put on a pair of leather trousers and a clean white shirt and joined the others to eat and discuss what we were going to do next. As well as sorting out Spiderwitch, now we had Maebh to deal with, too. I just hoped that they wouldn't find each other. Maebh wasn't the sharpest tool in the box, but Spiderwitch's cunning would more than make up for it. Spiderwitch would make big, fat bullets for Maebh to fire, if I knew Spiderwitch. At least we still had Master Theophilus Henbane under lock and key.

When we were assembled, the castle cook (now

cooperating, I was glad to discover!) brought us supper. The big windows let in the dying light, and the room was filled with a rosy glow. 'Red sky at night,' I said, enjoying the warmth on my face, 'and I don't mind a fine day now that Merlin's fixed the weather.'

'As long as it stays fixed,' Taliesin pointed out, spearing a chicken leg and dumping it on his plate. 'And since you mention Merlin, I think it would be a really good idea if you and Gwydion could try to be a bit tactful. He's had a bad couple of centuries lately, and –'

'Us, tactful! Us? Who was it broke the news to Flissy in a totally callous way? Who is it that keeps having tantrums? Not us, Taliesin,' I said.

'All the same, you know how short-tempered he is. If you could just try not to upset him, if we could all pull together, I'm sure we'd get the job done much more quickly.'

Well, there was sense in that, I suppose. All the same, Merlin was a pretty difficult character to get along with.

'We'll try,' I conceded. 'Won't we, Gwyd?'

'I'll try,' he said grimly. 'But I can't promise I'll succeed.'

Branwen came in, carrying a big dish of apples and cheese. She could barely see over the top, so I jumped up to take it from her.

'Thanks, Lady. Nearly dropping that, I was,' she grinned. Shoving a pigtail back over her shoulder, she turned to leave.

'Don't go, Branwen,' I called. 'Come and join us.'

Branwen's freckled face turned pink, but she tucked

herself onto the bench between T.A. and Nest and helped herself to a chicken leg.

T.A. was still quiet: partly grieving for Gwyddno and his wife, and partly smarting at being dumped by Elffin.

'Now.' I picked up an apple and sliced off a chunk of crumbly white cheese. 'What are we going to do about Spiderwitch?'

'Well, first we need to find her,' Taliesin pointed out, with his mouth full.

'It would be a help if we knew where to start looking,' I grumbled. 'When she just disappeared like that, it was dead annoying. You can't follow a person if you don't see which direction she goes in, can you?'

Branwen squeaked, and blushed pinker.

'What?' I said, putting down my knife. 'Do you know where she is?'

She shook her head. 'No, Lady. But Bugsy could find her for you. Bugsy said he can feel her when she's near.'

'He can?'

She nodded. 'So if Bugsy sort of flies around, then maybe he can find her. Then you can turn her into a bug and squash her, and Ynys Haf can be happy and peaceful and green again, can't it, Lady?'

'Something like that, Branwen,' I agreed. 'So, first we find Bugsy, I suppose.'

'I know where he is, Lady,' the little girl said. 'I can take you to him tomorrow.'

'I think we ought to go tonight, actually,' Gwydion put in. 'I have this weird feeling that if we wait until tomorrow it might be too late.'

'Too late for what?'

He shrugged. 'Don't know. But something tells me that the quicker we find her, the better.'

'You're the boss,' I said, finishing off my apple and popping a bit of cheese into my mouth after it.

'I am?' he said, with a mock air of surprise. 'Wow! Thanks, Tanz!'

To be quite honest, the very last thing I wanted to do was go dragon-hunting in the dark. No, I tell a lie. The VERY last thing I wanted to do was meet Spiderwitch. The second to last was go dragon-hunting. But you get the general idea.

All the same, Taliesin, Gwydion, Branwen and I gathered together on the battlements in the moonlight, and shifted.

Arms shimmered into orange-buff wings with pale undersides, faces flattened into white moon-shapes, noses turned into curved beaks, and four barn owls glided silently off the battlements in the cool night air.

What none of us knew was that Spiderwitch was entering a castle tower just as we were taking to the skies . . .

196

23

Gwydion and I kept Branwen between us for safety. She was a darker orange than the rest of us, but then, her hair was brighter, even than mine!

Her small owl-shape headed determinedly towards the mountains, her wings beating at twice the rate ours were, so determined was she to keep up with the grown-up owls. I hooted softly to Gwydion and Taliesin to slow them down: I didn't want to tire her out.

Bugsy was asleep when we found him, curled in a crimson ball in the moonlight, one great scaly wing covering his head and his mighty talons sheathed like a cat's claws. If it hadn't been for the horns, scales, fangs and size, he could have been a family pet curled up in front of the fire!

Branwen glided down and perched on his head. The rest of us perched on the rocks behind – it wouldn't be too bright, being in front of him when he woke, just in case he yawned: I didn't fancy being barbecued. I shifted Branwen first, and she sat, a skinny leg on each side of the giant head, completely fearless. The rest of us shimmered and stretched up and into our own shapes. The moon was so bright that it cast our shadows eerily. It was cold on the mountain, the first time it had been cold anywhere in Ynys Haf for months.

Branwen tucked a pigtail behind her ear, bent forward, and clouted the dragon hard on the nose with her clenched fist. I winced, and waited for him to erupt, roaring in fury, but Branwen knew what she was doing. It was probably the same for Bugsy as stroking my nose would have been if waking me. Not that stroking my nose would actually wake me: it usually took an earthquake, or Mam. Same thing, really!

The dragon twitched his cavernous nostrils. Branwen clobbered him again, slid down his neck and went round the front. This time he got one bleary eye open, and when he saw who had come calling, opened the other, grinned dopily, and raised a wobbly head. Branwen pressed her forehead against his, and the dragon listened. Then the great head swung round and surveyed us. We came round in front of him now that he'd seen us and wouldn't be startled. A mouth that burps a raging fire tends to make a person a bit cautious when approaching the front end.

'Bugsy says she's definitely in Ynys Haf,' Branwen reported. 'He felt her arrive, yesterday. He thought about finding her and frizzling her, but he was tired, so he thought he'd wait until tomorrow.'

'Where is she now?' Gwydion asked.

Branwen went head to head with Bugsy again. 'Close by, he says. And they are three,' she reported.

'Three?' I didn't like the sound of that.

'And he says that you're looking for her in the wrong place.'

'Well, I can see she isn't here,' I retorted. 'But does he know where the right place is?

'Of course. He says you will find her in the place that he once held safe for Gwydion Dragonking's noble father.'

Gwydion and I stared at each other. 'Castell y Ddraig!' he breathed. 'At least she hasn't tried to take

Castell Du. But what does he mean, there are three? I don't understand that bit.'

Neither did I. Then, suddenly, I had a horrible suspicion that I did. 'Oh, no!' I moaned. 'We know that Conor is still in the Land Beneath – at least, we hope he is. Maebh has probably found her by now – and the only other one possible, if it isn't Conor, is –'

'Henbane!' Taliesin and Gwydion said together.

'Exactly! And that could make things a leeeetle difficult,' I groaned.

Branwen walloped Bugsy between the eyes and punched him under the chin. The dragon closed his eyes in ecstasy. 'Not difficult for you, Lady,' she said stoutly. 'You can do anything. You can certainly beat that old spidery woman, you can!'

I was flattered by her confidence. I just wished I had a bit of it myself. Suddenly, the sharp moon-shadow in front of me blurred and faded as a cloud covered it. When the moon came out again, it was in front of us, not behind to cast our shadows. Now, I may be slow on the uptake, but even I knew that that was ever-so-slightly significant.

A single moonbeam, like the light of a very powerful torch, suddenly shone on Bugsy. The dragon looked up, the great head lifted to the light, sharp head-horns glinting. Something hanging round his neck on a golden chain gleamed. I bent forward and peered at it.

'What's that?' I asked, pointing.

Branwen touched her small forehead to the massive red scaly one. 'It's the Key,' she whispered.

'What key?' The object was the size and shape of a

rugby ball, and it shimmered in the moonlight. I couldn't understand why I hadn't noticed it earlier.

'Because he didn't want you to,' Branwen said, answering my unspoken question. Bugsy must be thought-reading me, too. 'It is the key to Gwydion's Dragonkingship,' the little girl replied, staring at Gwydion in awe. 'Bugsy says that Gwydion's father left it in his keeping when Gwydion was Dragonson. He said he may not have it until all he holds dear is at risk.'

'I think that sounds like now, Gwyd,' I murmured.

'But he can't have it yet,' Branwen said, as Gwydion reached out a hand to take it. 'Only the Lady Tan'ith may have it. Only the Lady may use it. And the Lady may only use it in the darkest hour of all, when it seems that all else has failed, and only then to preserve the Dragonking. Then,' she continued, 'when Ynys Haf is safe again, Gwydion Dragonking may have it. Only then will he be True High King.' She shook herself, the bright plaits whipping. 'Ooh, I *think* I got that right, Lady! Bugsy said I had to say 'zackly what he said.'

Gwydion and I stared at each other. 'Sounds like a secret weapon to me, Gwydion,' I said, my voice husky.

'Take it, my Lady Tan'ith,' he said.

Bugsy bowed his vast head to the ground and I carefully lifted the golden chain and guided it along the neck, over the horns and off his head. It was so big that if I'd hung it round my neck my head would have been dragging on the ground, but there are spells for that sort of thing. So I miniaturised it, and held in my hand a small, egg-shaped pendant that gleamed with a rainbow of colours, even in the moonlight. It was somewhere between opal and moonstone, but more beautiful than either.

I fastened it round my neck, where it lay snugly inside my jerkin beside the pendant Aunt Ant had given me for my thirteenth birthday so very long ago. It felt cool and hard, and comforting.

I plucked up my courage and gave Bugsy a friendly wallop on the forehead. 'Thanks, Bugsy.' The dragon bowed its head, gave Branwen a friendly nudge farewell, which made her stagger, and closed his eyes as if settling back to sleep. Then he opened them again and stretched out his head towards the little girl. They went head to head again, and she glanced quickly and me and Gwydion, and giggled.

'What?' I said, but she just giggled some more. I didn't press her: we had a battle to fight.

'Well, guys,' I said with a bravado I was far from feeling. 'I guess it's into battle again, right?'

Gwydion stretched, and the moon, now back in its right place, threw his long shadow across the mountain slope. 'And this time,' he said menacingly, 'we finish Spiderwitch once and for all. No messing about with mercy. This time, she dies.'

Well, I was impressed. Then he went and spoiled it.

'Hope so, anyway!' he said anxiously.

'Branwen,' I ordered, ignoring the last remark, 'you stay here with Bugsy until morning. If neither of us come for you, then he will take you back to your father.' I didn't add that, if neither of us came for her, it would be because we couldn't – for some reason or

201

another that I didn't particularly want to think about right then.

We shifted into three owls and circled once over Bugsy, the little girl tucked into the curve of his body, his wing arching protectively over both of them. Then we flew towards Castell y Ddraig, deep in the mountains.

The closer we got to the castle, the colder it got. I didn't think this was Merlin's work: I think this was the manifestation of all the evil that Spiderwitch and Henbane carried around inside themselves. It began to snow, and despite my feathers, I was shivering. I tried to 'think warm' and fluff my feathers, but it didn't work. There was snow on the peaks, and the battlements of the castle gleamed like a sinister wedding cake in the moonlight. Great fires burned in the courtyard, but even in the circle around the flames, the snow had not melted. We glided cautiously over the battlements, our sharp eyes watching for movement, but all was still. There seemed to be no army of any kind this time, which was one good thing, but then, Spiderwitch and Henbane together hardly needed mercenaries. I wasn't counting Maebh: she was nobody as far as magic was concerned. Light poured out of an arrowslit, colouring the snow a sickly yellow. I dropped silently onto the outside ledge and peered cautiously in.

Henbane, Maebh and Spiderwitch sat at a table, surrounded by what I first thought were curtains of coarse lacy stuff. And then I realised that it wasn't lace: it was a great mass of spiderwebs, filling the entire chamber except for the small space that the three of them occupied. Up in the shadowy roof-beams thousands and thousands of spiders of all shapes and sizes lurked and rustled, swift darknesses scuttling from strand to strand, torchlight casting their eerie, moving shadows on the walls.

Maebh, her beautiful face alight with malice, was leaning forward across the table watching what Spiderwitch was doing. From my vantage point at the arrowslit I couldn't see what it was, but I was willing to take a bet that she wasn't arranging flowers!

Then I realised that there was a fourth person in the room. He was smaller than the others and tightly bound in slender iron chains. His pointed face was sickly pale, the golden hair matted and lank, his magic completely wiped out by the iron.

She had Conor of the Land Beneath, and he was her prisoner.

Well, that was one good thing, right? He wasn't likely to take kindly to that, and if we could get him loose, then maybe he would come down on our side. Although I wasn't entirely sure, given the reputation of leprechauns in general, and Conor in particular – he was so crooked he could follow someone through a revolving door and still come out first – that he would ever come down on any side except his own. That was the way of it, and as O'Liam had told me often enough, a leprechaun cannot change its spots, so it would probably be better not to count on Conor for help.

I flew back to where the others were perched on the battlements, their beaks chattering with cold, and reported what I'd seen. Taliesin and Gwydion were huddled together for warmth, and I jostled them apart so that I could get between then, desperate to get some heat into my hollow bones.

'So, what should we do next?' I asked. 'I don't think it would be a good idea to just shift back to ourselves and barge in. But what will make the least impression on the atmosphere? After all, Spiderwitch can sense me when I'm around.'

'I've been thinking about that,' Gwydion said. 'I think you should stay out here and wait. If we don't come out after – oh, say an hour or two – then you come in and use that pendant thing that Bugsy gave you.'

'Oh, great idea, Gwyd,' I said sarcastically. 'Then, when you're dead and can't be High King anyway, I come along and zap the bad guys. If that's what this thing does. Could be it just vaporises Ynys Haf altogether so nobody can have it. We just don't know, do we? No, I'm coming too. The Three Musketeers, that's us. All for one, one for all, right? The question is, what shape should we change into?'

Of course, I knew.

24

I wished I hadn't thought of it, but I knew it was right.
And I made up my mind that, if I was going to be a
spider again, I was gonna be the biggest, hairiest,
spideriest spider that ever ran up a wall. There's a
story that Cardinal Wolsey was once scared stiff by a
huge house spider on a wall in Hampton Court, which
is why they are sometimes called Cardinal Spiders.
And if it was good enough to terrify a bloke that close
to the scary Henry VIII, it was good enough for me!

It takes a lot of concentration to shift into a large
spider: I think it's all those legs. Six is bad enough for
a person who normally only has two, but eight is like
trying to knit a sock with four pairs of needles. No,
I've never done that, either, but I can guess how
difficult it might be. We flew one by one to the
arrowslit, and with me going first, we changed
ourselves. First I had to squinch myself down – but
still retain my brain (for what it's worth) at full
capacity – sort of transistorise it. I'd come a long way
since I was turned into a limpet with a limpet-sized
brain! Then I had to concentrate on getting all eight
legs in the right order, sticking out of the right places,
and learn to scuttle without tangling them up. Oh, and
I also made sure I had a good pair of mandibles – big
enough to give a person a sharp bite if I had to. Then I
had to work out how to use my spinaret thingy, my
web-spinner, and then I waited for Gwydion and
Taliesin to do the same. When they were all spidered
up, I inspected them. If either one of them had scuttled

across my bedroom floor, I probably would have climbed straight up the wall and not come down, ever.

'Ready?' I whispered. They nodded, and we went in through the narrow slit in the wall. Then down the wall, across the floor, and onto a web that dangled alongside table. Up the web, scuttle, scuttle, until we were all high enough to see what Spiderwitch was doing.

She was holding the little doll representing Conor. She had stuck locks of his hair into the soft wax of the head, and fingernails into the ends of the stumpy arms, She had cut off a bit of his tunic and wrapped it round the doll, and she was currently adding the final touch – giving it Conor's small, pointed face. Conor, bound in iron and gagged, lay in the corner, his eyes wide with fear. Since he had taken the trouble to hide his hair-cuttings and nail-clippings in a silver-banded wooden box in a Time Door in the Black Castle of Ballygar, he knew exactly what Merch Corryn Du was up to – and what it meant for him. In front of her was a black and purple pincushion, shaped – inevitably, I suppose – like a tarantula, with black, beady eyes sticking out on stalks. It was filled with sharp, long pins . . .

She selected one, and poised it over the wax doll. She glanced up at Conor, her eyes narrowing behind the terrible red spectacles, as if selecting which part of him to hurt first. She raised the pin and stuck it into the doll's left leg. Conor yelled behind his gag and writhed in pain. Now, I didn't like Conor a lot (not at all, actually) but I didn't like to see anyone tortured for the fun of it.

'I have your attention now, do I not, Leprechaun?'

she purred. 'Listen to me well. I have you in my power, thanks to your kindness in leaving your little box where the GoodWitch could find it. When Gwydion Dragonking is dead, and the Lady with him, I shall not share Ynys Haf with you or anyone. I shall have it all. I shall be Dark Dragonqueen, the Dark Lady, and I shall rule here alone. It shall all be mine: the land, the people, the riches. I may let you live, Leprechaun, but cross me and you will die horribly.' To prove her point she gave the doll another little poke, and Conor writhed again.

And then I caught sight of Maebh's face. Watching her great-great-great granny work on the doll earlier, she had looked eager and enthusiastic. Now she looked faintly ill and definitely unhappy. I filed that away in the back of my spidery brain for future reference. Master Henbane, on the other hand, was thoroughly enjoying watching the leprechaun king wriggle.

'Oh,' he purred. 'Stick him again, your Spideryness! I love to see him suffer, I do indeed!'

But suddenly, Spiderwitch put the doll down and sat upright in her chair, her head on one side as if listening.

'Aaaaaaaah,' she hissed. 'Sssshhheeee is heeeeere!'

And I knew that she'd sensed me.

She stood up and sniffed the air. 'I can ssssssmell her! The GoodWitch is close, so close!'

Since I was about a foot above her head, she didn't know how close. Suddenly her eye lit on a black beetle scurrying across the chamber floor. She raised her foot and crushed it. 'Ha!' she crowed, then frowned. 'No. That was not you, was it, Witch? Ssssshow yourself. Where are you, GoodWitch? Are you too much of a coward to face me?'

Now, if I'd been Wonderwoman, I'd have materialised in front of her and said 'Here I am! Do your worst!' Did I do that? Do you think I'm *stupid*? No, don't answer that. Of course I didn't. In fact it was all I could do to stop myself backing up the web another couple of miles. All my common sense was saying, 'Get out of here, Tanz, while you still can'. But the rest of me wasn't listening.

Gwydion and Taliesin, like me, were motionless black shapes poised on the web. She was looking straight at us, but perhaps she couldn't imagine that we'd ever change to her own shape . . .

I sent a thought wave: *what are we going to do now, you two?*

Scream and faint? Gwydion's thoughts came back.

Ha, ha, very funny. Not. Look, we can't fight here. We have to wait until she leaves the room. Too many webs to tangle us up in. No, we wait and we watch. When she goes outside, then we follow. As soon as we can't get tangled in her webs, then we'll shift and finish her, I sent back.

Once her back was turned, I took the opportunity to scuttle up high in the web out of sight, and the others followed. The roof-beams were full of spiders of all sorts, Merch Corryn Du's courtiers, all of them: trapdoor spiders; crab spiders; zebras, daddy-long-legs; wolf spiders, mesh-webs, tiny money-spiders; garden spiders with their distinctive white crosses on their backs, all scuttling and dangling and spinning

208

intricate and deadly patterns. There was no bustle of conversation, no sense of community or togetherness: each spider was a separate, lethal entity. And Gwydion and Taliesin and I sat amongst them, practising spinning long threads of sticky gossamer, praying that we could get away before any of them spotted that we weren't very good at it and got suspicious.

At last, Spiderwitch stopped stamping on beetles and trapping flies in a vain search for me, and flounced out of the door, closely followed by Maebh and Henbane, who aimed a kick at Conor's leg as he passed. If looks could kill, the one Conor gave him would have shrivelled his shoelaces.

We followed them down the spiral staircase, and into the Great Hall. Gwydion's chair of state was still on its dais, with my smaller one beside it (mental note: get that fixed. I want one the same size, Gwyd!). The three of us scrambled up a nearby curtain and kept very still.

Spiderwitch strode onto the raised wooden platform and plonked herself down in Gwydion's chair. Henbane lifted his dark robe and scuttled after her, poising his behind over the seat of my chair. However, just as he was about to lower himself into it, Spiderwitch shoved it away, and Henbane sat down, hard, on the floor.

'You presume, Henbane!' she hissed. 'How dare you? You are not of the blood royal. Maebh –'

Maebh, shaking her black curls, blushed and dimpled and tripped forward, all ready to sit beside her grandmother.

'– you, Maebh, have the blood, but not the brain.

No, I shall sit here alone. You are not worthy, either of you. I need no one else.'

Henbane clasped his hands under his chin. 'Whatever you wish, Great Majesty. I live only to serve you,' he smarmed, simpering. 'Whatever I can do to assist, is it not my duty to do it, so?'

'It is indeed,' Spiderwitch purred. 'Fetch food.'

Henbane inclined his head obediently. 'What is your desire, Majesty?'

Spiderwitch put her head back and closed her eyes. Her mouth curved, and the pointed teeth showed. 'Some nice – fat – fresh – bees. The furry, stripy sort. With cream. And honey. Thick, thick cream and runny honey. Otherwise their nasty little legs tickle my throat as I swallow them.'

Henbane scuttled off to fetch them and Maebh slumped sulkily on a stool at Spiderwitch's feet.

Now that was altogether too much. I remembered the glass tank full of bumble bees that had been in her chamber in the Land Beneath: I was determined she shouldn't enjoy her horrible snack in MY land!

Without thinking twice I dropped off the curtain, shifting on the way down. In the back of my mind I heard Gwydion and Taliesin send thought waves – *not yet, Tanz!* but ignored them. No way was Spiderwitch eating bees while I was around.

Spiderwitch's eyes were still closed, but Maebh saw me instantly.

'Granny!' she shrieked, 'Oh, Granny, the GoodWitch is here, she is so!'

Spiderwitch's eyes shot open, and she jumped to her feet, the chair of state crashing backwards. 'At last!' she hissed. 'Oh, now I have you! And all alone, I see. Good. I can pick you off one at a time. So much easier for me. So much less *taxing.*' She wagged her finger, roguishly. 'I'm not getting any younger, you know!'

'And if it's anything to do with me, you won't get any older, you nasty old bat,' I said.

She winced. 'So rude. I shall have to punish you for that. Ah, Henbane. As you see, our friend has arrived.'

Henbane, struggling under the weight of an enormous tank of bumble bees – which I was glad to see still had all their wings intact – tottered into the hall. 'Ah, and so she is, Glorious Victorious one,' he burbled. 'Are you going to smite her?'

'Oh, yes, Granny. Smite her, smite her!' Maebh chortled.

'You've got a short memory, Maebh,' I said sternly, beginning to wonder why Gwydion and Taliesin were still spidering it in safety while I was down here in danger of getting zapped. 'Gwydion and I saved your life, twice. Talk about ungrateful. *And* I broke my promise to Conor of the Land Beneath for your sake and didn't hand you over to him.'

She looked faintly guilty, but not a lot. 'Whatever you did, I owe all my allegiance to my dear Granny. Granny loves me, don't you Granny? You are going to let me be Queen sometimes, aren't you? And I shall be Queen forever when you die.'

'Whatever gave you the idea that I shall die?' Spiderwitch asked. 'You're much too stupid to rule anything. If you're lucky I'll marry you off to someone. Otherwise I shall dispose of you.'

'Granny! How could you? Do you not love me at all?'

Spiderwitch folded her arms and glowered through her hideous red lenses. 'No. Not at all. I don't love anyone. Never did. Wasteful emotion, love. In fact, I don't really see the point of keeping you around. You've made a mess of just about everything.'

Just while I was distracted by Maebh dissolving into a sobbing heap on the floor, Spiderwitch threw a spell at me. A big, splattery, ugly, terminal spell . . .

25

Well, terminal if it had hit me, that is. One thing a coward learns really fast is when to duck, and I make no bones about it, I'm a coward.

'Missed!' I chortled as the wall-hanging behind me burst into roaring flames. I collected myself, riffled through the spells in the black end of the Emerald Spellorium, and hurled a particularly nasty toe-nail curler at her. She batted it back, and while I was scuttling out of its way, chucked a thunderbolt that bounced off the wall and out through the arrowslit. And still Gwydion and Taliesin hadn't come to back me up.

Where are you? I thought at them. *Shouldn't you be helping me a bit down here?*

I didn't expect the reply I got. Gwydion's frantic voice spoke in my mind:

We can't! Merch Corryn Du has enchanted us! We can't shift! And the other spiders have cottoned on to us! No time to talk, Tanz! You're on your own for a while!

Oh, great. Now I had to fight Spiderwitch alone, and my back up force was surrounded by hordes of hostile arachnids! I risked a glance upward. The spidery throng was moving like a black tide towards Gwydion and Taliesin at the centre of the web . . .

No time to worry about them – Spiderwitch drew herself up to her full height and closed her eyes. She flung her arms up over her head and purple flames shot from the ends of her fingers. Then she opened her eyes and glared at me, her eyes gleaming with malice behind the awful red glasses. She stretched out her arm, the long crimson fingernails like hideous red beetles as she pointed at me. Fire gushed from her finger-ends and licked at my boots. I jumped back, just in time, and hit her with a storm-cloud that broke over her head and drenched her. All her fire went out, and the coil of black hair on top of her head began to unwind. Water dripped off her nose and her dress clung to her bony frame. She bared her pointed teeth, and I could tell she was just a tiny bit annoyed.

Suddenly she shivered, shimmered, and became a scorpion, scuttling across the floor towards me, sinister sting quivering. I leapt over it, just as she shifted back to herself, and found myself nose to nose with Henbane, still clutching the tank of bees. I struck upwards at the lid, it flew off, and a torrent of amber and black insects poured out, filling the room and buzzing around Spiderwitch. While I was at it, I zapped Henbane, knocking him unconscious with a small thunderbolt to keep him out of my way. As soon as this was over, I intended to un-magic him, once and for all. Right then, though, Spiderwitch was more than enough for me to handle.

'Don't sting her!' I yelled to the bees. 'Get away while you can!' I knew that a bee would die for every sting inflicted, the barb torn out of its living body. I couldn't sacrifice bees, no matter how dire my straits were, and right then they didn't look particularly good.

Obediently, the bees poured out of the arrowslit – at least they were saved. Then I turned my attention back to my enemy.

She hurled a small black cloud at me, which expanded in mid-air and became a net of spiderweb gossamer. It floated above me like a parachute, and I knew that if it landed on me, I was probably finished. From the look of it I could tell it wasn't just a web: she'd added a deadly ingredient somehow. I shifted into a mouse and shot behind a tapestry which burst into flames just as I shot out the other end, a second burst of flame missing my twitching nose by inches.

Two could play at that game, however. I magicked a sack – behind Spiderwitch – and dropped it over her head. She struggled, blinded for a second, but then the sack fell limp and empty to the floor and a large tarantula scuttled out. And then the tarantula shimmered and grew.

And grew.

And grew. And I was looking at the real Merch Corryn Du. She was a giant spider, twice as tall as me, great mandibles clashing in the air, hairy legs like tree branches supporting the long body and blunt thorax of a wolf spider. Wolf spiders don't hang around in webs waiting for their prey to come to them: they hunt it down on foot, and I was it!

For an instant I was paralysed with terror. To see a spider that big looming over a person is to know what real fear is. Cardinal Wolsey would have dropped dead on the spot, trust me. Then it got worse. A loop of silk shot from her spinarets, and wrapped itself around my legs. She caught hold of the end and began to reel me in like a fish on the end of a line, towards those gnashing jaws. I tried to think of a spell to free me, but my mind was a blank.

This was it, then. The way it all ended. One bite and I was dead and done for, and Gwydion and Taliesin would get killed and eaten by the other spiders, and Merch Corryn Du would rule Ynys Haf. I'd failed. My boots slithered on the floor as I tried to pull away, my arms windmilling as I tried to keep my balance, but it was useless. I crashed to the wooden floor, sliding closer, closer, to those awful, venomous jaws. Spiderwitch's red eyes flashed in triumph. I clasped my hands to my chest and tried to think of a good prayer – and before I even had time to think of one, it was answered.

Under my jerkin, I felt something oval and hard.

I dived my hand down inside my collar and hauled at the chain. It snagged on the inside of my jerkin, but another tug freed it.

I waved it under her nose and suddenly she stopped pulling. Her eyes grew wide. Maebh shrieked.

'Granny! Look out, Granny! She's got the Dragon's Tear!'

Is that what it was? Well, whatever its name was, it was dead handy to have around, I can tell you.

The monstrous spider backed away, its front legs waving, as if it were trying to push even the sight of the Dragon's Tear away. The jewel suddenly began to glow: it shone emerald as the cover of the Spellorium, then turned the eerie, silvery blue of moonlight. Brighter and brighter it became, and then, when I was beginning to wonder if it would blind me before it did whatever it was supposed to do, it began to throb with power at the end of its chain. It began like a heartbeat, a slow dub-dub, dub-dub. Then it got louder and louder until it seemed to become part of my body, all of me vibrating with the pulsating power of the Dragon's Tear. My hand shook with the effort of holding it out towards her. The noise filled the room, vibrating the very air I breathed, and I clenched my teeth and concentrated on hanging on to consciousness as blackness filled the room.

Spiderwitch screamed in agony, a haunting inhuman screech. Then she began to melt like a lolly in a rainstorm. Her eight legs dissolved into puddles of black, sticky stuff where they touched the floor. Lower and lower she sank, her whole body shimmering as she desperately tried to find a shape that would get her out of the danger she was in, but it was useless. Half-spider, half Spiderwitch, she writhed and shrieked, but still she sank and sank until only her red eyes gleamed frantically and the terrible mandibles clashed on empty air. Then there was silence.

The Dragon's Tear winked out as if it had been switched off. The ugly black pool began to shrink, all that remained of Merch Corryn Du evaporating before my eyes, until nothing at all was left of her.

Two spiders detached themselves from the web above my head and abseiled down on their own silk. I looked up at the ceiling and saw that every other spider had stopped moving. They were frozen, watching as their terrible Queen was finally and completely vanquished. Forever.

Taliesin and Gwydion shimmered and shifted, Spiderwitch's spell on them released by her death, and my friends stood beside me. Above our heads the vast army of spiders rustled eerily as, large and small, they retreated out of windows and doors and into holes and cracks and floorboards, a black, sinister flow, until the room was empty except for us. And Henbane and Maebh.

Maebh, seeing her Granny destroyed, was sobbing in a corner, and I could tell that she'd be no further trouble at all. Henbane, on the other hand, was pretending to be still unconscious, but I'd seen the glint of a half-opened eye and knew he was faking it. Before he could do anything I grabbed Gwydion and Taliesin's hands and, our magic powerfully joined, repeated the spell that removed every trace of his magical powers. When it was done, he was just an unpleasant, greasy little man, who slunk and slithered out of the door and out of the castle and into obscurity.

It was finally over.

*   *   *

Well, it was and it wasn't, if you see what I mean.

We had to sort out Conor of the Land Beneath, but the way that turned out was quite weird. He was very subdued, especially when we let him know that we had the wax doll that Spiderwitch had made. I locked it in the wood and silver box and gave it to Merlin to look after. Conor knew we had complete control over him from then on, so he had to behave. With that insurance for his good behaviour, we let him go back to Erin to rule his people, and wonder of wonders, Maebh went with him, which meant in a roundabout way, I'd kept my promise. She decided it would be better to marry him, and be Queen of the Land Beneath, than not be Queen of anything.

Gwydion and I made a final trip to Erin, stopping on the way to make a pilgrimage to the ravaged land of Cantre'r Gwaelod. We stood on the cliffs and threw garlands of flowers into the waters and said silent prayers for all who had died.

Then, it was off to keep my promise to Big Deirdre. She hadn't done much, but at least we hadn't been attacked by the Banshee or Pwca Horse or anything, and I still felt sort of sorry for her. Her reward? Well, you remember the Black Castle of Ballygar? We confiscated Deirdre's poor cub's head from Conor's trophy wall, and took it to Ballygar to reunite it with his body, although when he'd got it back he had to carry it under his arm rather than wear it. It wasn't in the rules to re-attach it, apparently. Then Big Deirdre moved in as caretaker, so she sort of had her Babby back, and her cub had his Mammy, and even though they couldn't do much in the way of cuddling and stuff, they were both a whole lot happier and the poor cub stopped crying for her. Last I heard, the Bog Fairy had moved into Deirdre's cottage and taken over her job as Guardian of the Port. Still hoping to catch O'Liam on his way back in, I suppose.

Not a hope there, mind. Once we were back in Ynys Haf we gave O'Liam and Siobhan the best wedding we could. The bride, who had luckily left Cantre'r Gwaelod before the flood, wore white with emerald ribbons, and O'Liam was in a red suit with green boots (naturally!). Branwen was bridesmaid and was horribly sick with excitement and too many ice-cream sundaes. Brigid kept her Light Fingers in her pocket for the night, although when she finally returned to the Land Beneath we noticed that there were some spoons missing. We had a wonderful feast, with all O'Liam's favourite foods, a wild ceilidh afterwards with Conor's musicians, sent over for the occasion, and for once O'Liam was so happy he couldn't think of a single saying.

Merlin could, however. 'Women,' he warned O'Liam darkly, 'keep their tongues in their pockets until they marry.' Which considering what happened to him a century or two later, is quite funny. He never was good at taking his own advice. There was a girl called Nimue at the wedding as a matter of fact. No one admitted to inviting her, though Aunty Fliss had a somewhat guilty look about her when I mentioned it. Merlin and Nimue seemed to hit it off . . . But that's another story.

When everyone had gone to bed, and O'Liam and Siobhan Flowerface had ridden off into the sunset, so to speak, Gwydion and I were left alone. We climbed to the battlements of Castell Du (Castell y Ddraig needed de-spidering and spring-cleaning of a whole lot of webs), looking out across the peaceful, green, happy Island of Summer. Corn waved golden in fields and silver rivers leapt with salmon, and smoke rose from the roofs of the village houses through the trees.

'Don't go back, Tanz,' he begged, gathering me into his arms and kissing my nose. 'I need you.' I nestled my head against his chest, feeling utterly miserable. I didn't want to go back. It would have been so easy to have stayed there, and become Dragonqueen straight away and forgotten about the Other Time. But I knew it wouldn't be right for me.

'I've got to go back, Gwyd. I need to go to college.'

'No, you don't. You've got all the education you need already. No one knows more about Ynys Haf than the Lady.'

'Ynys Haf, yes. But I don't know enough about people yet. I don't know about politics, or history, or justice, or any of the other stuff that people need to be good rulers and keep their people happy. And if I'm going to be your Dragonqueen, Gwydion, I need to know loads more than I do now. I'm not just going to be a dressed-up doll at your side. I'm going to rule with you. I'm the Lady in my own right, after all.'

He was silent. 'But you will come back, won't you? You promise?'

I looked up into his dear face. 'Of course I will. I belong here as much as you do. Besides,' I thumped his arm, hard, 'there's a legend, isn't there? Something about the second daughter of the seventh daughter of the two-hundred and seventy-seventh generation of the Daughters of the Moon being Queen to the two-hundred and twenty-second Dragonking of Ynys Haf? Can't fight that, Gwyd. I'll be back.'

But there was a lump in my throat big enough to choke a camel: I wouldn't see him again for years and years. What if he found someone else in the meantime? I knew now that sometimes the little details in a legend can be changed. Sometimes all it takes to change an age-old story is a pretty face . . .

*　　　*　　　*

Much to my surprise, I did well enough in my A levels to get a place at Aberystwyth, and T.A. did, too. Different courses, mind, she's much brainier than me.

I was going to do Welsh History and Welsh Literature; she was doing Latin and Law. Scary stuff.

On Going Off to University day, we went together in convoy, T.A. and her Mam in their car, me and my Mam and Dad in ours. We did all the boring stuff you have to do when you start, then went to see where we'd be living for the next year, in Halls at Waunfawr, overlooking Cardigan Bay. If I squinted my eyes, I could almost imagine the lost, lovely land of Cantre'r Gwaelod, out there . . . Elffin turned up safe and sound, by the way, although a little blighted by thwarted love. Served him right, dumping T.A. like that.

We unloaded into our respective rooms, other people bustling about moving in too, boys as well as girls. Because both Mam and Dad were helping me, it took me longer to move in (you wait: you'll find out!) so T.A. picked up a box of crockery and food and stuff (Mam was sure I'd starve to death without her) and took it into the communal kitchen to help me.

Seconds later, there came the sound of breaking china.

Mam and I looked at each other. I rolled my eyes. 'Woolworths, here we come,' I sighed.

'Go and see how much damage she's done, Tanz,' Mam begged. 'I can't bear to look!'

T.A. was standing in the doorway, her mouth open, shattered china all over the floor. 'You're never going to believe this, Tanz,' she whispered, her eyes wide.

I looked past her.

A familiar figure sat at the kitchen table, eating buttered toast and Marmite from a huge jar.

'Want some toast?' a familiar voice said. 'Name's Gwydion Ddraig-Brenin. Just moved in downstairs. Doing Welsh History and Politics.'

A grin spread over my face as the clear, green, cat-like eyes met mine, and white teeth flashed in a dark, humorous face.

I think my grin probably met round the back of my head!

Here end the Books of Tanith.
What next?
Wait and see . . .

Acknowledgements

O'Liam of the Green Boots is very grateful (and so am I) for:

> *A Little Book of Irish Sayings* illustrated by Jon Berkeley (Appletree Press)

and

> *The Irish Phrase-Book* compiled by Diarmuid Donnchadha (Mercier Press)